Blood Reckoning

C. M. Sutter

AUTHOR'S NOTE

This book is a work of fiction by C. M. Sutter. Names, characters, places, and incidents are products of the author's imagination or are used solely for entertainment. Any resemblance to actual events or persons, living or dead, is entirely coincidental.

The scanning, uploading, and distribution of this book via the internet or any other means without the permission of the publisher is illegal and punishable by law. Please purchase only authorized electronic editions, and do not participate in or encourage electronic piracy of copyrighted materials. Your support of the author's rights is appreciated.

ABOUT THE AUTHOR

C. M. Sutter is a crime fiction writer who resides in Florida, although she is originally from California.

She is a member of over fifty writing groups and book clubs. In addition to writing, she enjoys spending time with her family and dog, and you'll often find her writing in airports and on planes as she flies from state to state on family visits.

She is an art enthusiast and loves to create gourd birdhouses, pebble art, and handmade soaps. Gardening, bicycling, fishing, and traveling are a few of her favorite pastimes.

C.M. Sutter

http://cmsutter.com/

Contact C. M. Sutter - http://cmsutter.com/contact/

Blood Reckoning
FBI Agent Jade Monroe - Live or Die Series, Book 3

What should be a lazy Saturday for Agent Jade Monroe turns out to be anything but. Wakened by an urgent call from her partner, she's told that she won't have the day off after all— five homeless people have been murdered overnight.

Days later, five more people are found murdered, including the daughter of Milwaukee's mayor. Police discover that every victim had a loved one with connections to the mayor himself. Finding out why becomes a daunting task, and nobody in the mayor's circle is talking.

Is there a murder cover-up in play, and if so, what does it have to do with Mayor Kent, a member of both Milwaukee's upper echelon and one of the most wealthy families in the state?

The answers will come, but at what cost? Jade has to solve the murders, but doing so will involve the biggest risk of her life.

See all of C. M. Sutter's books at:
http://cmsutter.com/available-books/

Find C. M. Sutter on Facebook at:
https://www.facebook.com/cmsutterauthor/

Don't want to miss C. M. Sutter's next release?
Sign up for the VIP e-mail list at:
http://cmsutter.com/newsletter/

Chapter 1

The warehouse had been abandoned for years. Had it been located in an area of Milwaukee that anyone cared about, the people who came and went during the late-night hours would have raised a red flag, but they didn't. The city's cream-colored brick building had seen better days, and the structure was an accident waiting to happen, yet the Condemned and No Trespassing signs at every point of entry went unheeded.

The working class who'd lived near the defunct manufacturing neighborhood twenty years earlier had long ago moved on to different jobs and greener pastures. Homeless and derelict people occupied the few blocks, along with some who were there for a private meeting.

Fires for light and warmth burned in fifty-gallon drums scattered throughout the lower level. The regulars arrived at the warehouse to introduce their recruits to Jacob and Evelyn, the leaders of the group. They'd chosen Milwaukee's rebels, those who had committed crimes throughout the city in the name of the greater good. The recruits were the ones who'd vowed to help expose the city's hypocrites, the worst offenders of them all, and they intended to make good on that promise.

Pallets had been stacked into a makeshift stage and stood several feet higher than the cracked concrete floor below.

Several recruits sat cross-legged three feet from the stage, and standing at their backs were the people who had convinced them to help expose the true criminals of society.

From the darkened rear of the building, a man and a woman entered the room and stepped up to the stage. They welcomed the recruits and thanked them for wanting to help right the wrongs they'd encountered.

The recruits would have to prove themselves worthy before joining the final and most important mission. Because no one was allowed to speak of the group—including where they congregated, who they were with, or why they were there— the final mission would be revealed at a later date.

The plan had been in the works for some time and was near completion. Once every *i* was dotted and every *t* crossed, the takedown would be implemented. Targets would be identified in several phases, and Jacob and Evelyn insisted they had undeniable proof that those people needed to die. The tasks would be difficult and dangerous to complete, and they needed extra help to ensure the mission's success.

Each recruit drew an identical knife and envelope from a basket that was passed around. Inside the envelopes were instructions that they needed to complete as part of their initiation, a way to prove they were loyal to the cause. If successful, they would be given one more task—a daring one—and upon its completion, the final and most dangerous mission would take place.

Jacob spoke up. "I want every recruit to complete the instructions as written on the note inside the envelope they chose. Open your envelope and read the instructions now. This will be your one and only opportunity to leave the group without consequences. Speak up if you can't complete the task laid out in the instructions. The task needs to take place tonight with photo proof of its completion presented to us tomorrow." He nodded. "Go ahead. Read your task and tell me your decision." He pointed at the person on his far left. "What's your answer?"

The recruit nodded. "I'm on board."

"Good. Next?" Jacob questioned the remaining recruits, and only one said he couldn't go through with the instructions. Jacob tipped his head toward the door, giving the person standing at the recruit's back the cue to remove him from the room.

The recruit stood and was led out of the building.

Evelyn folded her hands, whispered a prayer for success, and asked everyone to leave. It was time for the recruits to go out, prove themselves, then return the next day to share their stories with the others.

Chapter 2

I loved Saturdays when I wasn't on the road. I would lie in my comfy bed until the aroma of freshly brewed coffee and sizzling bacon drew me out like a magnet. Amber enjoyed cooking, and her culinary expertise was definitely one reason that I appreciated the fact that my sister lived with me and hadn't mentioned getting her own place over the past four years. The same was true for Kate. She was our dearest friend and a great sounding board, especially since she had that sixth sense, her uncanny psychic detective abilities. She had solved many crimes with that gift, and all the people who'd scoffed at her skills years ago were now true believers. Kate was also a neat freak, and that was a godsend in our hectic lives since we were always on the go. Luckily, our shared cat, Spaz, was self-sufficient, and as long as he had his favorite kibbles and a fresh bowl of water, he was good to go.

When I heard Amber's bedroom door open and close, I smiled. That meant breakfast would be ready in a half hour, and I could dreamily remain in bed for another thirty minutes. Just as I dozed off again, my phone rang.

I groaned before lifting my head off the pillow. "You have to be kidding!" I snatched my phone from the nightstand and checked the time before answering. I was fully prepared to give a telemarketer an earful, but these days, even the telemarketers used nothing but robocalls. I could still yell into the phone, but the satisfaction of telling someone off just wasn't the same. It was only seven forty-five, which would normally irritate the heck out of me, especially on a Saturday morning, but when I saw the name on the screen, I knew it had to be important.

"Renz, what's up?"

"Sorry to bother you on what could have been a peaceful Saturday."

"What *could* have been, meaning it won't be?"

"Yeah, I'm not liking the idea of working on a rare Saturday off any more than you are, but there's been several disturbing discoveries overnight."

After sitting up in bed, I thanked Amber with a nod. She'd just brought me a cup of coffee, placed it on the nightstand, and walked out. I assumed she heard my phone ring and figured it was a work-related call.

I took a much-needed sip of the brew before continuing. "So what are the disturbing discoveries?"

"Five bodies were found by homeless people this morning."

I raised my brows. Having five people die in Milwaukee in one night wasn't unusual, and that was especially true if they were all homeless. Many homeless people were drug abusers, and they were easily taken advantage of and beaten to death or died of disease, illness, starvation, or weather exposure.

"So the bodies were found around the camps?"

"Sounds that way, at least in the general area."

"Right, and why should we be involved? The homeless aren't usually the healthiest of people to begin with."

Renz let out a long groan. "Because every one of them had their throats slashed."

I was stunned and had to process what he'd just told me. "You did say these bodies were found in different areas, didn't you?"

"I did. So either one person was pretty busy all night, or there were multiple killers. When I say scattered around, I don't mean within blocks of each other. They were found throughout Milwaukee County, and that covers a lot of territory."

"Wow. It almost sounds like a coordinated attack."

"We can't get ahead of ourselves, but we do need to get to the office. Taft is being briefed by the sheriff since every victim was found in a different police district. Deputies and officers are at each scene and have already reported in to their direct supervisors. The bodies haven't been moved, and considering the quantity and manner of death, local law enforcement thought it prudent to get ahold of Taft. We're considering these deaths as serial crimes, and even though the murders may not have been done by one hand, the totality of it still falls in that category."

"Because it could have been a group effort?"

"Yes, and no matter if one person held the knife or three,

because the manner was the same, the murders themselves would count as a serial crime. There's no way five homeless people killed on the same night in the same way is a coincidence."

I had to agree. "Okay, I should be at the office within an hour. At least traffic won't be an issue today." I hung up and dove into the shower for a quick rinse. Within ten minutes, I was dressed and had my hair sleeked back into a ponytail. I yelled down the hallway to Amber that all I needed was a travel cup of coffee and a bagel. I would have to forego that delicious breakfast she was preparing, but if I was lucky, I could snag a strip of bacon on my way out the door.

Thankful that it was Saturday, I wouldn't have to give Taft the typical traffic excuses I usually gave for my late arrival.

After passing through the gate in that one-hour time frame I had promised Renz, I dropped off my briefcase, and because our shared office was empty, I assumed he was there and either grabbing a coffee or already in the conference room. I headed there since I still had coffee in my travel cup.

I found everyone from our team seated around the table, and because I had the farthest to drive and it was an unscheduled meeting, nobody gave me that "you're late again" headshake. We were all on board and ready to get busy, especially since we had five murders to deal with at once.

I wasn't worried about what I'd missed. Renz would update me if needed. All Taft said she knew was that the people who reported the crimes were also homeless and had been dumpster diving or milling around the area that morning when they came upon the individuals. They found the nearest person with a phone, or the nearest store that was open, and asked them to call 911. The descriptions of the deceased were all the same—one long and deep slash across the neck. The victim had no chance of survival and likely bled out immediately.

"Did any of the callers know or recognize the victims?" I asked.

Maureen shook her head. "I don't have that information yet. What's most important at this moment is to have Dave establish times of death for each victim to see if there actually was a way that one person could have committed the crimes. Yet the estimated TOD is often too broad to really narrow down if one killer could move about the county fast enough, find victims to target, complete the act, and then do that four more times within that time frame Dave gives us."

David Mann—or just Dave, as he preferred—was the medical examiner for Milwaukee County and had been for years. I was sure he and his team would have their work cut out for them on this case.

"Has Dave gone to any of the scenes yet?" Fay asked.

"He's been to two of them, and so far, he's said the neck injuries were relatively the same—ear-to-ear slashes. There weren't any other wounds visible, but he said he'd know more after the bodies were on the autopsy tables and washed down thoroughly."

I grimaced. "I'd imagine besides the time of death, Dave should be able to tell if the slashes were the same depth, were done using the same amount of force, and if the fatal injuries were done left to right or right to left. That would tell us if the perp was one and the same."

"And so would the actual wound," Renz said. "If the same person committed every crime, then he'd likely use the same knife, wouldn't you think?"

Maureen cocked her head. "That depends and could go several ways. If he wants us to think different people were responsible, he may use a variety of knives, or if several people actually were responsible, they may all buy identical knives. I'd trust the depth of the wounds as well as the right or left motion before I'd trust the blade type. Personal mannerisms can't be altered as easily as knife types can."

Maureen had a point, and we would have to wait for the autopsy reports before we knew how many killers we were dealing with.

"Do homeless people even carry identification, and does law enforcement know the victims' names yet?" Charlotte asked.

"The police have started canvassing the area, but I want all of you there too. We'll be the lead if these murders are actually connected. You'll go to the crime scenes, track down the callers—the police or deputies can point them out—and then ask those people and other residents at the camps if they knew the deceased by name. Press them. Homeless people have a way of clamming up. They prefer to be left alone. If any of the vics did have IDs, that'll help speed up our ability to notify their next of kin."

I huffed. "If the next of kin even want to be involved. Many times, homeless people have been ostracized by their family. They're deemed as outcasts."

Maureen agreed. "That's true, but we'll do the best we can."

Renz took his turn. "So divide up and hit every crime scene?"

"Yes. I have the addresses here, and you guys can decide who goes where." Maureen slid the printed reports to us, and Renz passed them out.

"Jade and I will go to the two scenes where Dave and his team have already been since there's only four sets of us and five crime scenes."

"Okay. Head out, then, and keep me posted."

Chapter 3

That morning, the recruits were led into the same building as the night before. They sat on chairs placed in a semicircle, and the man and woman were also seated and facing them from several feet away.

Evelyn took the lead by welcoming them back. She said she was excited to find out how the previous night had gone and wanted to hear everyone's story. After that, they would have one more task to complete before the bigger plan would be revealed—along with why it had to occur.

Brandon was asked to start. The note in his envelope had told him to go to the tent city south of downtown, where the homeless had set up camp beneath the freeway overpass. His instructions were to find the shelter of a homeless person who was farthest from the main group—someone literally on the fringe—and slit their throat from ear to ear. Jacob and Evelyn needed photo evidence and details of the killing until the moment that the victim took his or her last breath.

Jacob and Evelyn were particularly interested in Brandon. Brandon had mentioned to his recruiter that he wanted to be a part of something, and that information was passed on to Jacob and Evelyn. He'd said that being in a group of likeminded individuals, people he could identify with, was the answer to his dreams. Jacob had learned that Brandon had prior offenses, so the kid was just the type of person they sought. He was an outspoken hater of many, a friend to few, and was passionate about exacting justice on those who deserved it. He'd said it made him feel alive, and all he needed was something to belong to. He'd found what he was looking for with Jacob and Evelyn.

"Tell us everything in detail, Brandon," Jacob said. "Spare nothing."

After taking a deep breath, Brandon began. "I went to the location the note said to go to and found the homeless camp. There were about thirty tents and makeshift cardboard shelters. It was two in the morning, so only a few people were milling around. With my head down, I picked up my pace, got around them without being noticed, and didn't make a peep. I needed to locate my target."

"Good call," Jacob said. "You don't want anyone to be able to identify you, even though most of those people are druggies and don't live in reality." He tipped his head. "Go on."

"I continued until I was at the last few shelters. Out of the corner of my eye, I saw movement, so I followed from a distance. It was a woman who was walking to a tent, I assume after taking a piss. Hers was the last tent, exactly what I needed. She bent down to crawl inside, and I grabbed her from behind, cupped my hand over her mouth, and dragged her away." He went on. "She put up a good fight, kicking and flailing, but I like the fight. It revs me up, you know?"

The group nodded. After all, homeless people were disposable and the perfect practice subjects.

"Then what?" Evelyn leaned forward, clearly focused on his story.

"After I dragged her about a hundred feet from the camp, I saw an alley that was lined on both sides with dumpsters. I wedged her and myself between two of them so she couldn't kick anymore, flicked open my knife, and pulled her head back. That's when I sliced her." His eyes widened. "The damn blood squirted so far it hit the brick wall and ran down it. I even took a picture of that." Brandon passed his phone from one recruit to the next and finally to Jacob and Evelyn. It was a job well-done.

"So nobody saw you, and she didn't scream?" Jacob asked.

"Nope. Easy as pie."

Evelyn caught Jacob's attention with a subtle head tip.

He stood and turned to the back of the building, and she followed. "Give us five minutes, people. We'll be right back." Once they were out of earshot, Jacob asked why she'd pulled him aside.

"It's Brandon. He has the enthusiasm and bravery that we need as a leader. I'm sure the others did as they were instructed, but Brandon seems to be in a league of his own. I think he's capable of being our second in charge."

"He's not even twenty-one, and you'd trust him over the

others who have been in our group from the beginning? I don't want to cause jealousy or any bad blood between our helpers."

"Just keep it in mind. I'd say he's at least on equal ground with Erik."

"Really?"

Evelyn nodded and took Jacob by the hand. "Let's get back to the meeting. I want to hear the other stories."

After returning to their seats, Jacob and Evelyn continued with the other recruits, listened to similar stories, and viewed proof of the acts through cell phone pictures. Everyone seemed trustworthy and willing to move on to the second task.

"Are any of you left-handed?" Evelyn asked.

They all shook their heads.

"That's even better. I like the idea of making this hard on the police and the city officials. The medical examiner won't have anything to differentiate one killing from another, and all of you completed your tasks between two and two fifteen a.m.?"

They said that they had.

"Okay, that's all for now, and I'm pleased with your dedication. Those homeless people were your easy targets. It's unfortunate that they're throwaways, but nobody cares about them, and they won't be missed. Jesus will take them into his fold. Now, we need all the knives back, and then you can go about your day. Your recruiter will be in touch soon with the second assignment."

After the knives were collected, the recruits were escorted out.

Chapter 4

At the first scene Renz and I went to, an officer walked us to the body. I knew from the police report that the victim would be a woman who, according to Dave's best guess, looked to be around fifty. He didn't find an ID on her, and the police said there wasn't one in her tent either.

When we reached the alley, the deputy guarding the scene lifted the blood-soaked sheet and exposed the woman's body. She was lying between two dumpsters, her legs buckled behind her and her head resting abnormally on her left shoulder. I'd grown used to seeing dead bodies over the years, but that never made it easier. I furrowed my brow, knelt, and gave her a long, hard look. I pointed out the inside of her elbows, which revealed scarred skin and recent track marks.

"She's a junkie. It always boggles my mind how they get access to the drugs. They can't afford to clean themselves up or eat right, but there's always money for drugs, alcohol, and smokes." I pushed off my knee and stood then swapped places with Renz so he could take a look.

"They're resilient, Jade, and find ways, whether it's by

sexual favors, robbing people, or stealing food and bartering for their drug of choice."

"I know, but it still makes me sad. I mean, where's their family?"

"Unfortunately, that's the million-dollar question. This woman will get her autopsy and then likely be buried in the county cemetery as a Jane Doe. Let's go take a look at her tent and talk to the person who discovered her."

We walked to the cluster of tents, and the officer directed us to the green one just beyond the end of the overpass. The constant rumble of cars, trucks, and semis passing above us was louder than I'd imagined. Even if our Jane Doe had fought for her life, her struggles would have probably been drowned out by the noise. Yet if Dave determined that her death occurred late at night, the traffic would have been substantially lighter. Still gloved, I pushed aside her dome tent's flap and crawled in. Directly to my left sat a small tote, and opposite that was her makeshift bed. It consisted of two tattered blankets on top of three-inch-thick stacked cardboard. Its purpose was likely twofold—to provide a cushion and to ward off the cold dampness of the pavement beneath the tent. I felt a twinge of guilt as I recalled lazily lying in the comfort of my clean, cushy bed only hours earlier. I turned around and opened the tote. Renz excused himself and squeezed in next to me.

"What's in there?"

"Don't know. I'm just about to open it."

Renz pointed with his chin. "Go ahead."

As I lifted off the lid, he illuminated the tote with his

phone's flashlight. Inside were several cans of pork and beans, a bag of potato chips, a half-eaten jar of peanut butter, two pair of sweatpants, two T-shirts, one open pack of menthol cigarettes with a lighter inside and six unopened packs, and four dollars in change that had fallen to the bottom of the bin.

I'd never been in a homeless camp, let alone in one of the tents, to actually see how few worldly possessions those people had. This woman's possessions boiled down to a small amount of food, a few items of clothing, her much-needed cigarettes, and what I assumed was an uncomfortable bed of sorts. Some homeless people probably had it better, and some had it worse.

I turned to Renz and shook my head. "Why don't these people just stay in shelters? And then what happens when the temps fall below zero?"

"They figure it out or freeze to death. Many build barrel fires and huddle around them to stay warm."

"But why—"

"Why don't they move indoors?"

"Yeah."

"Because outliers don't want rules imposed on them. They aren't the down-and-out types who just need a handout and a clean bed to sleep on for a while. These are the diehards who won't abide by rules set by establishments that are there to help them. The shelters have rules, and the residents can't have drugs or alcohol inside. There are curfews they have to abide by, too, so they choose to tough it out rather than cave in."

"That's a real shame, and obviously, by what happened overnight, a dangerous life too." When I noticed people waiting to grab what few items the deceased woman owned and her tent as well, I shook my head. "What do we do with this stuff?"

Renz shrugged. "There's nothing in the tent that leads to her identity, and it doesn't look like anyone rifled through it. I'd be fine with letting the other homeless take what they want. Why guard a tent that doesn't have any forensic value? We don't even know who her next of kin is to call."

I agreed, yet the whole scene reminded me of vultures waiting for their chance at roadkill. I needed to stop thinking about the sad reality and focus on the murder itself and why she in particular was the target. I waved down the officer who had taken us to the body. "Who found her?"

He pointed at a man six tents farther in under the overpass.

"He's been interviewed?"

"Yes, but he seemed real fidgety, like he was coming down from something."

"Sure. We'll interview him again anyway. Anyone else?"

"Nope, but there were a few people up and about during that time according to Mr. Fidgety. He might be able to shed some light on that."

"Okay, thanks."

Renz and I walked over to the man whose eyes darted back and forth as he sat on an advertising crate next to his cardboard shelter. He was one of the lucky ones to have his "home" under the overpass since rain and snow would definitely turn his cardboard into mush in no time. We approached cautiously, not wanting to give him a reason to clam up, yet we didn't know if anything he told us would be credible.

"Hello, sir," I said as we neared. "We hear you're the one who found that woman between the dumpsters this morning. Can you tell us about that?"

"I told that guy." He pointed at a random police officer, and we knew he hadn't spoken with the man.

I played along. "Yes you did, but he can't remember what you said. I'll write it down, though, because your story is very important to us. What's your name?"

"Ray. My story is important?"

"Of course it is, Ray," I said. "Right now, you're the man of the hour."

"I am?"

I nodded and gave him my best smile then pulled my notepad and pen from my pocket. "I'm ready whenever you are."

"I need a cigarette first. Do you have one?"

I gave Renz a side-eyed glance and stood. "I'll be right back." I rushed to the woman's tent, grabbed all the packs of cigarettes to use as bargaining chips, and returned to the man's campsite. "How about a brand-new pack of smokes?"

In a flash, he tried to snatch the pack out of my hand.

"Hey, hey, not so fast, buddy. You'll get one now and the rest of the pack after we hear your story. Deal?"

He squinted as he sized me up. "Two now and then I'll talk."

"Okay, two it is and eighteen more later." I opened the pack and pulled out two.

With shaky fingers, he fished a lighter out of his pocket, took the cigarettes from me, and lit one. The end glowed orange as he drew in a mouthful of nicotine.

"Go ahead," Renz said. "We need to hear everything you know."

The man blew out a puff of smoke then pointed toward the alley. "I heard it back there last night, but I sure as hell wasn't going to see what the commotion was about. I knew it couldn't be anything good, and even though my life sucks, at least I'm alive."

"Ray, wasn't the freeway noise too loud to hear anything?" I squatted to his level and leaned in closer.

He looked past us as if watching his memory play out on the big screen. He pointed over his shoulder. "The fellas down there were yacking among themselves and didn't hear what I heard, and at that time of night, it's quieter than now."

"And what you heard was?"

"A scuffle, muffled cries, and then a dragging sound on the pavement. I crawled out of my box to take a look, but they were too far away. I couldn't make out anything except dark figures moving into the alley, and then I heard noises at the dumpsters." He stuck a shaky finger in my face. "I'm at those dumpsters all the time, and I know the sounds they make. It wasn't long before everything was dead quiet again. I never saw anyone coming or going after that, so I crawled back in my box and stayed perfectly still. I didn't want to be seen or heard—just in case."

"Understood," Renz said.

I jotted down everything Ray had said then asked about the time. "Do you have any idea when you heard those sounds?"

"Only because of the bells."

I looked around for a steeple and saw it. "The church bells?"

He nodded. "Ding-dong, ding-dong."

"So two in the morning?"

He nodded again.

"We heard that you didn't crawl out of your box again until this morning."

He shook his head vigorously as if he wanted to rattle away the memories. "Nope. I didn't show my face until the sun was up and it looked safe. I waited until more people were moving around before I went to the alley to see if anything was there to explain the noises I heard."

"And that's when you saw her?"

He looked at me, squashed the first cigarette under his worn-out sneaker, and lit the second one. "I'll admit, I haven't run full speed in five years, but I did then. I went to that quick shop on the corner over there"—he jerked his head to the left—"and told them to call the cops. When they showed up, I took them to her body."

"How did you know she was dead?"

He stared off into space. "Because there was so much blood, even on the brick walls."

"Did you know the woman by name? Have you ever talked to her?"

"Nope. She kept to herself, and that's probably why she pitched her tent farther out. Big mistake, big mistake."

I frowned. "Why do you say that?"

"She hasn't been here long—only a few weeks. Nobody from our camp knew her, so the killer isn't one of us. We're all in the same boat with nothing worth a shit, so why bother?"

"That's true," I said.

"What's your opinion?" Renz asked.

He wagged his finger. "I'd say a stranger was out looking for trouble and just happened by her tent. That woman was an easy target being on the edge of the camp like that."

Renz rubbed his chin. "But how would a passerby know it was a woman in that tent?"

Ray shrugged then continued. "People take pisses at night, you know, especially if they don't want an audience. They go find a dark spot and drop their drawers. Maybe he saw her and followed her back to the tent."

I tipped my head. "Makes sense." I pointed at other people milling around. "Anyone else see anything besides you? Was there anybody near the alley this morning?"

"Nope, and there wasn't talk from the others of anyone hearing noises last night."

"Okay." I pushed off my knee and stood. "Here's my card, Ray. I know you don't have your own phone, but if something strange comes up, go to that corner store and call me. Here are the cigarettes I promised you." I handed him the pack and noticed several missing teeth as he formed a wide smile.

"Much obliged"—he looked at the card—"Agent Jade Monroe."

I glanced at the woman's tent as we passed it. The camp's residents had already emptied the contents and were now arguing over possession of the tent. I wondered how life had gotten so bad for so many people. Homeless settlements were everywhere and in all major cities across the country.

"Earth to Jade."

I looked at Renz. "What?"

"I asked if you were ready to go to the second location."

"Oh, yeah. Are we supposed to say something to that deputy at the dumpster?"

"Like what?"

"Like we're done and they can release the body to the nearest hospital's morgue until Dave has them all delivered to the medical examiner's office."

"I'll call Taft, and she can arrange that with the local police chief or the sheriff."

I sighed. "Okay, and I'll look over the second police report while you drive."

Chapter 5

Renz clicked off the update call to Taft just as we got back to our car. The second site we were headed to was a vacant lot and only feet from a public sidewalk. The police report mentioned a woman by the name of Terry Gerhart who had made the 911 call.

I paraphrased the report as Renz drove. "Okay, sounds like a deceased male was lying in a vacant lot between two run-down buildings. Apparently, this Terry Gerhart told police she was going to the gas station to pick up a quart of milk when, from the back seat, her daughter yelled out that there was a man lying on the ground. Terry stopped, backed up to make sure her daughter hadn't mistaken a bag of trash for a man, and she hadn't. That's when Terry called 911 from her cell phone. The police told her to wait there and said they were en route. The report shows they arrived four minutes later. They describe the man as someone possibly in his fifties, disheveled, and wearing ragged clothing. They also said they were aware of a homeless camp that was set up in a park two blocks away, and the man might have come from there."

"And the cause of death?"

Even though we were already aware that five people had been found with their throats slashed open, I groaned. "Yep. Same as the woman at the dumpster—throat sliced open from ear to ear."

It didn't take long to reach the location since it was a ten-minute drive from the first site. Renz parked in front of the vacant lot, right behind a Milwaukee police car. The body, still lying in the lot, was surrounded by a portable shield, and yellow police tape blocked that area of the sidewalk from pedestrians.

We showed our IDs to the officer at the sidewalk, ducked under the tape, then sidestepped the garbage strewn around the lot. The officer, a D. Todd, stood at the body. Renz gave him a nod, then we looked over the barricade. The man lay faceup with his eyes and mouth wide open. His neck was wide open, too, and his severed esophagus was exposed.

"Damn." I cringed as I looked at the results of the brutality the man had suffered. I turned away and addressed Officer Todd. "Do you have the address of the woman who called 911?"

"Yes, ma'am, and we also have the location of the park where the homeless camp is set up."

"Good. Any ID on the man?" Renz asked.

"The medical examiner checked earlier and emptied the man's pockets into an evidence bag. It's in my squad car for safekeeping until we release the crime scene back to the neighborhood."

Renz tipped his head toward the street. "We'll need to take a look at that evidence."

"Sure thing." Officer Todd yelled out to the officer who stood at the crime scene tape. "These agents need to see what's in that evidence bag."

We thanked him and joined the policeman at the trunk of their squad car. I pulled a pair of gloves from my pocket, and Renz gloved up too. He opened the bag, reached in, and pulled out the laminated ID card. The rest of the items consisted of a few dollar bills, change, an unopened pack of cigarettes, and a key ring with a four-leaf clover on it.

I shook my head and pointed at the charm. "Guess that didn't do shit to bring him luck."

Renz pulled out his phone, took a picture of the ID, then dropped it back into the bag. He thanked the officer, and we returned to our car to go pay a visit to Terry Gerhart and the homeless camp.

"So what was the guy's name?"

"Leonard Roche, age fifty-five, with an address that's probably not valid anymore. This ten-year ID card expires in a few months."

"Let's check out the address anyway."

"We will, but that address isn't going anywhere. Let's talk to Mrs. Gerhart and some of the residents at the camp first."

Renz drove the three blocks to the Gerhart home. After parking along the curb, we took the sidewalk to the front door of the stucco-and-brick Tudor-style home, and Renz gave it two knuckle raps. We had no idea if anyone would be there or not since we hadn't warned that we were coming. Just as Renz reached up to knock again, we heard someone approaching the door. I sighed with relief that we would get the interview over with and wouldn't have to circle back a second time.

The door opened all of six inches, and we could see only half of a woman's face. "Can I help you?"

A girl who looked to be around seven peered out from behind her mom.

The woman spun. "Poppy, get inside!"

We already had our badges in hand, and I took the lead. "Mrs. Gerhart?"

"That's me, and it looks like you're the FBI. Why on earth are you here?"

"The incident earlier in the vacant lot—"

"It was a man who had passed away, so I called 911. That's all I know. It isn't like I walked up to him or knew who he was. For God's sake, my daughter was in the car."

I gave her an understanding smile. "If we could have a few minutes of your time. I promise it won't take long." I wondered why she was being less than cooperative. We weren't there to accuse her of anything. "Please?"

She let out what sounded like an annoyed huff then came out and stood on the porch. She pointed at the bench that sat under the eaves. "Have a seat and please make this brief. My daughter has been crying ever since we got home."

"I'm sorry—"

"You don't understand."

It was more than clear that we didn't, and I wanted to

know why she was being short with us. "Do you have a problem with law enforcement, Mrs. Gerhart?"

"No, but I have a problem with my daughter reliving her father's death. It was Poppy who found my husband lying in the backyard. He had fallen off the ladder while cleaning out the gutters, sustained a serious head injury, and died the next day. That was only two months ago." Her eyes pooled with tears. "Poppy still has nightmares. Please, just ask your questions so I can get back inside."

Renz took over. "We're sorry for your loss, ma'am."

She nodded for him to move along.

"Okay, did you see anyone at all in that lot other than the deceased man?"

"No, it was probably too early for people to be out and about. I was going to make pancakes for breakfast when I realized we were out of milk, and that's the only reason I was out at that hour. I was headed to the gas station's quick mart since it was the closest place to pick up emergency items. Usually on Saturdays, Poppy and I have breakfast, relax in front of the TV, and do nothing until around ten."

"And the time you went out?"

She rubbed her forehead. "It was seven or so, give or take a few minutes." She looked toward the door. "Anything else?"

"Is that gas station open twenty-four hours a day?" I asked.

"The pumps are, but the inside closes at two a.m. and reopens at six."

"Okay, and you waited at the scene until the police showed up, correct?"

"Yes, and I told them what I just told you. There wasn't anything else to say."

I stood and pulled a card from my pocket. "There are county-run grief programs available to you and your daughter, Mrs. Gerhart."

"I know, and I'm considering that."

"Here's my card in case anything else comes to mind. Thank you for your time." Back at the car, I climbed in and fastened my belt. "Guess you never understand why people behave the way they do until you know their story."

"And that was a sad story for sure. So, are you ready to continue on?"

"Yep. We need to get to the bottom of those killings, and the TOD is crucial in knowing if there was one killer or more."

We headed back the way we'd come, then several blocks farther south, we reached Iroquois Park. A good fifty or more tents were set up there, and I was surprised to learn that so many homeless people lived outside of city-run shelters. As a North Bend resident for my entire life, and usually working cases in other states, I'd never had a reason to be in areas of Milwaukee where homelessness was prevalent. If there were incidents where law enforcement was needed, the local police jurisdiction took care of those issues. The only reason we were called in was because we were the serial crimes unit.

"Where should we begin?" I asked.

Renz shook his head. "At tent one, I guess. We'll show Leonard's ID photo to everyone and see if anybody owns up to knowing him. Homeless people are squirmy around uniformed cops, but maybe because we're in street clothes, we'll look somewhat harmless."

I pointed at the yellow and green tent. "Might as well start there. Either they recognize the picture, or they don't."

"Or they say they don't when they really do, but then we wouldn't know the difference."

"So we have a fifty-fifty chance of hearing the truth, but in my opinion, and with the lot being only a few blocks away, there's more than a fifty percent chance that Mr. Roche lived in this camp."

We struck out with the first dozen people. Either they shied away and wouldn't talk to us at all, they told us to get lost, or they were too wasted to answer coherently. I had a feeling people were going to be less than cooperative, then we got to a dirty red tent. A woman sat outside on a folding chair and stared off to her right.

"Excuse us, ma'am," I said, causing her to jump. "I'm sorry I frightened you, but we have a picture I'd like you to look at."

"No time." She waved her hands in our direction. "Go away. I'm too busy."

I frowned. "Busy doing what?"

"Waiting for Lenny. He's been gone too long, and I can't go out and look for him. Someone will steal our stuff, and it'll all be gone when I get back. People are bad." She shook her head. "Real bad."

We had to show her the picture of Leonard's ID since it was obvious that we'd found the person we needed to talk to. We just had to get her focused on what we were about to say.

Renz handed his phone to me, and I inched closer to the frantic woman. "Ma'am, I have a picture here. Is this Lenny?"

"What? Why would you have a picture of Lenny?"

"Is this him, ma'am?" I turned Renz's phone around and handed it to her.

She stared at the photo. "How did you know that Lenny was my husband?"

"We didn't. We've been showing his photo to everyone. May we sit for a minute and talk to you?"

She nodded at the ground. "Grab a seat."

Renz and I sat on the tarp that covered an eight-by-eight section of pavement in front of her tent.

"So where is Lenny? Did he get lost or arrested for something?" She squinted at us with suspicion in her eyes. "I know you're cops no matter how much you church up your uniform."

I wanted to smile at her feisty words, but the situation didn't call for it. I sucked in a deep breath before continuing. "Where was Lenny going this morning?"

"Nowhere. He left last night to get me smokes. I couldn't sleep, and I wanted cigarettes, but he never came back."

"Where did Lenny go for the cigarettes?"

"To the gas station. There's a bar that's closer, but they won't let our type inside."

"What's your name?" Renz asked.

"Mary, Mary Roche. So did you arrest Lenny for something? We're always being hassled by the cops."

"No, ma'am. I'm sorry to tell you this, but a woman driving by spotted Lenny in a vacant lot this morning."

"And? Did he fall asleep out there?"

"No, ma'am. He's dead."

Mary let out a gut-wrenching scream and buried her face in her hands. I noticed the dirt under her fingernails and had to look away.

"How, why? Lenny wasn't old, so how did he end up dead? What am I supposed to do now without my Lenny?"

"Mary, I think you should stay in a shelter. It's safer there." A cold breeze swirled around my neck. "And winter is right around the corner."

Renz picked up where I left off. "Is there anyone in particular at the camp that Lenny didn't get along with?"

She coughed through her words. "Everyone got along the same—not good and not bad—just getting by the best we can. Are you saying somebody killed him?"

I nodded. "That's exactly what we're saying, and I'm sorry for your loss. Did you see anyone follow Lenny when he left last night?"

"No, no, no. People mill around all hours of the night, and I wasn't paying attention. I just wanted my damn cigarettes. It's all my fault, and because of that, my husband is dead."

She was right, but if it hadn't been Lenny, I had a feeling anyone walking the area at that time of night would have been the victim. My gut said the killings weren't specific to anyone, just random acts of opportunity.

"Do you have a friend in the camp? Somebody who'll give you moral support in your time of need?"

She shook her head.

"Okay, then I'll make a call on your behalf. You'd be better off in a shelter, and I'll try to find one close by." I gave her my card and a hand squeeze, and we walked away.

Chapter 6

As they sat side by side in their living room, Evelyn and Jacob reviewed every sheet of paper they'd spread out in front of them. It was time to put the second phase into motion. They were getting close to that final moment where everything they had planned came together.

"The recruits did well and have proven themselves worthy to move on to the next step, one that's even riskier." Evelyn lifted the sheet of paper containing the names and smiled. "They can take care of the next group tonight. When we finally get to the people responsible, my heart will rejoice when we rid them from the earth. An eye for an eye as far as I'm concerned. We'll look each one in the face and tell them why they're about to take their final breath. Their family will finally learn the truth—the real truth, not a covered-up lie. They'll understand the agony we went through because they'll go through it too."

Jacob added his opinion. "Our pain was and still is beyond horrible, yet they dismissed us, said we were mistaken and had made things up. We had no proof of wrongdoing, but when it's all said and done, we'll come through victorious."

Evelyn wiped her eyes. "But it still won't bring them back."

Jacob reached out and squeezed her hand. "It won't, but it'll be a victory nonetheless." He took the sheet of paper out of Evelyn's hand and circled the top five names. "We'll have our members follow them throughout the day, see what their routines are like, and then the recruits can take action tonight. They'll have completed their work and proven themselves brave and capable, but they'll have to stand down unless we need them again. Who knows? There may be more people to eliminate if this situation snowballs."

Evelyn frowned. "You mean law enforcement?"

"I mean anyone who gets in our way."

Chapter 7

"Let's head in. I'm sure by now, the rest of the team has seen the other bodies, talked to the police, and spoken with people in the area. They've probably gone back to headquarters already."

"Sounds like a plan." I searched my phone as Renz drove.

"Whatcha looking for?"

"A contact name at a nearby shelter. Hopefully, they'll talk to Mary and convince her to stay there, at least for the winter months. It won't be long before the snow is flying."

Renz looked up. "Yep, and once the sky takes on that winter-gray hue, it doesn't change again until April."

"Thanks for that image. Winter is already too long and too cold, but why does it have to be gray too?"

Renz pulled a quarter out of the console tray. "Don't know, but here's a quarter."

I grinned. "Yeah, and what am I supposed to do with that?"

"Call a weatherman. He might have the answer to your question."

I cleared my throat. "Excuse me? First, I don't think pay phones exist anymore, and second, you should have said 'weatherperson' since the meteorologist I watch on my favorite news channel happens to be a female."

I punched his shoulder, and Renz laughed. "Sorry. I keep forgetting we live in the twenty-first century."

"Okay, I think I found somebody who can help Mary, so shush while I make the call."

We were back at our St. Francis headquarters twenty minutes later. I looked out at Lake Michigan as Renz pulled into our parking spot. The water looked cold and uninviting, and other than a barge along the horizon, I didn't see a single boat.

Once on our floor and after seeing that every office was empty, we grabbed our coffee cups and headed to the conference room. There was always a pot of fresh coffee when we had updates and brainstorming sessions. Renz and I entered and found everyone from our team back and seated. Each agent gave us a quick update of the site they went to, and most were repeats. There were no witnesses to the brutal killings, and all the victims appeared to be from homeless camps.

We went over our findings with the group. The first victim, a female around fifty, had no identification, so she would be considered a Jane Doe unless someone who actually knew her name came forward. I explained that we did have a witness of sorts—the man who called 911 and went by the name Ray. We went over his account of hearing sounds in the night and seeing shadows moving toward the alley.

"He remembered the church bells ringing twice."

"So two in the morning?" Taft asked.

"That's correct, ma'am. Ray admitted to being afraid, so he didn't wander out until after daylight when other people were up and about. He told us he recognized dumpster sounds from the night before and went to investigate. That's when he found the body, ran to the corner market, and had them call 911."

Maureen raised a brow. "Did he recognize the woman?"

Renz took over. "He said he did and knew which tent she lived in. His opinion was that she was a victim of a crime of opportunity for the perp since her tent was the farthest from the rest. He assumed the killer saw an easy target and chose her as his victim."

I added my two cents. "Ray said she had only lived at the camp for a few weeks and kept to herself, so that's why nobody knew her name. We searched her tent and found a little bit of food, a couple of T-shirts and two pair of pants, cigarettes, and some change at the bottom of her tote. Nothing of importance."

Taft tipped her chin after taking notes. "Okay, and the second location?"

"We actually found the wife of the victim at Iroquois Park, where a homeless camp is set up. The deceased did have an ID, and that, along with a few other items, was collected in an evidence bag. I took a picture of the ID, and then we went from tent to tent until we came upon the wife. She was worried sick. Said her husband, Lenny, had left the night before to go to the gas station to buy her cigarettes.

38

The gas station closes at two a.m."

Tommy asked about the cigarettes. "So did he have a new pack of cigarettes on his person?"

I sighed. "He did, but we didn't tell the wife that. She felt guilty enough."

"So that means he was killed right after two o'clock and was heading back to the camp."

Renz nodded. "That's what we concluded and what would make the most sense."

"His name?" Taft asked.

"Leonard Roche. I called the nearest shelter, and they have room for the wife, Mary. They said they'd send somebody out to talk to her."

"Good. Sounds like those two murders were purely crimes of opportunity. Neither victim was targeted in particular. What about the rest of you? Any evidence that the murder victims were deliberately chosen?"

Everyone shrugged and said that after interviewing people who knew the victims, not one could think of anyone who'd had a problem with them.

Fay brought up a good point. "So we now know that two of the victims were killed around two a.m., and we'll learn the approximate TOD on the other three as soon as Dave reports in with his rigor and temperature analysis. What if the person who died was completely irrelevant and it was more about the timing?"

I felt my eyebrows shoot up. "Well, knowing that Leonard and Jane Doe were killed at roughly the same time and the locations were ten minutes apart by car, then there has to be more than one person committing the murders."

Kyle cocked his head. "Or they aren't connected at all. Maybe slitting throats is the latest method killers are fond of. It could be a new trend among the depraved because it's a quiet act."

"That's also a possibility, but at least we're throwing out ideas," Charlotte said. "If the time of death is what we're supposed to notice, then it was absolutely a coordinated plan of attack. The killers"—she air quoted the plural word—"want us to know there's more than one of them, and the only way to do that is by killing all five victims in a scattered area at the same time."

Taft reached for the landline phone. "I need to ask Dave if he has TOD estimates yet, and they have to be as precise as possible."

While Taft made the call, I started scratching out a list of questions to field to our team. We needed to know if there were hate groups who might be suspects. Were there people who hated the homeless or the space they took up in our cities? Could tourism be affected? Safety? Maybe even organizations who fought drug and alcohol abuse were angry. The sanitation department would have to be involved and possibly restaurant owners whose businesses could be failing because homeless camps took up sidewalk space right outside their eateries. Maybe that sidewalk space could have been used for outdoor dining. The list went on and on, and we had a lot of work ahead of us.

Maureen hung up minutes later and told us Dave's initial findings. According to body temperatures and the amount of rigor setting in, he had put the TOD for the other three within the same parameters as the two Renz and I saw—between midnight and four a.m. That wasn't good enough. We were sure about the time of our victims' deaths, and we needed more, as in video evidence or witness statements at the other scenes in order to know if the time of death was the same for all five people. We had our work cut out for us, and we had to consider the citywide police jurisdictions and the county sheriff's office too. I could see the number of officials involved causing the investigation to go sideways fast. It was something Maureen said she would address. She said she'd also try to get Dave to tighten the time frame once he had the victims in the autopsy room and under ideal conditions for examination.

I brought up the hate-group idea to check the temperature of the others, and they all thought it could be a possibility. By picking out one homeless person to kill from each camp, the message was coming across loud and clear—homeless camps weren't wanted in the city, but finding the individuals or group responsible would be a challenge.

I addressed Maureen. "We do have a nationwide database of hate groups, don't we?"

"We do, and that would be a good starting point."

Over the next hour, we narrowed down the most likely group of people who would be affected by the homeless camps. We came up with restaurant owners and safety and sanitation committees as the people most likely to be hurt financially and physically by the homeless presence. There weren't specific hate groups in those businesses, and getting angry at the possible lost revenue and unsightliness and then turning to murder was quite a jump, but people had killed for less. We needed to put feet on the ground and interview restaurant owners near camps and talk to authorities in the city's safety and sanitation department.

I brought up my own thoughts before we were tasked with those assignments. "Wouldn't our work be more productive at specific locations? I'd think police detectives would be able to speak with restaurant owners and sanitation departments. That way, each branch of law enforcement would have a particular task to follow through with and wouldn't have overlapping duties or step on each other's feet."

Taft rubbed her forehead. "You're probably right. I want all of you to return to the crime scenes you were at earlier. Look for store cameras, PODs, anything in a three-block area of the murder that might be of help. Talk to more people too. By the time you're back, Dave will probably have a tighter time frame of when the victims died. If you're able to review camera footage, look specifically for suspicious activity between one and three o'clock in the morning."

Chapter 8

Renz turned right and pulled into a drive-through restaurant, ordered two grilled chicken sandwich meals with iced tea, and moved ahead.

"Must have been reading my mind," I joked.

"Nope, I heard your stomach growl."

"Guess it is way past lunchtime."

"Yep, and I'm starving too. We might be out until after dark, so we may as well eat something while we're stuck in the car anyway."

"Damn, Renz. Who knew you had such a brilliant multitasking mind?"

He shot me the middle finger, lifted his hip, and pulled out his wallet. "There's a lot you don't know about me, Monroe."

"Pray tell."

He wagged his finger. "I'm saving that for the time we're enjoying a beer or a glass of wine at a bar that isn't connected to a hotel, remember?"

"Ah, that's right."

Renz paid for our meals, passed the bag and drinks to

me, then pulled out of the lot. I unwrapped our sandwiches, handed one to him, then opened the console and placed his bag of fries and the iced tea inside.

"That's what consoles are for?"

"Not exactly, but it works, doesn't it?"

He bit into his sandwich, nodded, and continued on.

We arrived at the overpass a half hour later with a different task to work on. We were looking for buildings in the area that might have a camera facing the overpass. I assumed they would have to be commercial buildings or possibly parking structures.

"What's your take on PODs? Does this area warrant them?" I asked.

"I'd say so, but that's probably something the police department would check into."

"Do we have a point person at the PD that we're supposed to work with? The chief, a handful of detectives, or who?"

"That's a tough one since the crime scenes are all in different police jurisdictions."

"Then we need a liaison for each location. We should talk to Taft about that," I said.

We parked in the same area we had been at earlier and climbed out of the car. Renz opened the back door and looked around. "Do we have binos in here?"

"They're in the trunk along with the vests."

Luckily, we found three sets of binoculars. We pulled out two, slung them around our necks, and walked to the area between the alley where our Jane Doe was killed and the spot where her tent had sat that morning. With the binos against our eyes, we looked in every direction for wall-mounted cameras on buildings. Renz walked closer to the freeway entrance, and I stayed put. We were both doing slow spins when I heard somebody call my name. I turned and saw Ray walking toward me.

"You came back, Agent Jade. Why?"

I chuckled at the name. "We're looking for cameras that might have caught the person who took the woman into the alley."

"But it was really dark last night, and like I said before, I only saw shadows."

"I know, but it's something we need to do."

"The cops are all gone, and so is the body. Otherwise, I would have told them."

I frowned. "Told them what?"

"About the man who was milling around here an hour ago. He doesn't live in the camp, and there's nothing to do in this area, so why be here at all?"

"Hmm… was he passing through like this area was a shortcut to go somewhere else?"

"No. He stood pretty close to where you are now, looked back at the camp, and then turned down the alley."

"The alley where the dead woman was? That alley?"

"Yes, Agent Jade. That alley."

I squeezed his arm. "Did he see you watching him?"

"No, ma'am. I was standing behind an overpass pillar."

"Come with me." We walked to where Renz was standing. He had moved closer to the freeway and still had the binos up to his eyes. I cupped my hand to my mouth and yelled out due to the traffic noise. "Renz!"

He turned, pulled back at the sight of Ray, then walked toward us. "Ray, what's going on?"

"Tell Agent Lorenzo what you told me."

Ray repeated the information.

"Did you get a good look at the guy?"

Ray closed his eyes and nodded. "Good enough to recognize him if I saw him again."

Renz gave us a thumbs-up then pointed at a building north of us. "It's broad daylight now, and I just spotted a camera on top of that bank building." He jerked his head. "Up for a coffee, Ray?"

"Coffee? I haven't had coffee since—well, I don't know how long it's been."

"Come on. It's too noisy here, and it's cold outside. I think that coffee shop I saw three blocks away will do just fine."

"Are we going in a cop car?"

"It's a dark sedan," I said, "but it has a scanner and a police radio inside."

Ray rubbed his hands together. "I've never been in a cop car before."

Renz patted him on the back. "And that's a good thing, Ray, but this is a special occasion."

After Renz parked in front of the coffee shop, I lifted my briefcase out of the back seat. Inside, I always kept notebooks with lined and unlined pages, pens, pencils, erasers, and a recorder. That was a habit I'd picked up after meeting Kate years back. She always had the items necessary to draw, take notes, and record other people's accounts at length. Sometimes, she would pass the notebook to them and let them jot down their own memories. Later, when she was alone, she would decipher what it all meant.

At the coffee shop, we were shown to a booth and sat down. Renz ordered a carafe of coffee, three cups, and a double cheeseburger with fries for Ray. I smiled at his generosity, opened my briefcase, and pulled out a lined notebook and a pen. After our coffee arrived and the waitress walked away, I asked Ray for a description of the curious man.

I watched as Ray poured three packets of sugar into his coffee along with enough cream to turn the brew nearly white. "You set?"

He nodded. "I'm ready when you are, Agent Jade."

I smiled. "Good deal. So how far away from the man were you?"

He rubbed his chin. "He moved around a lot."

"Okay, then the closest you were at any point to him?"

He stared at the fluorescent ceiling lights. "Forty feet. Yeah, that sounds right, forty feet."

"That isn't bad, and from that distance, you probably got a decent look at him, right?"

Ray tapped his fingers on the table. "Yeah, yeah, but let me tell you quick before it fades away."

"Go for it," Renz said.

"He wasn't old. Under twenty-five, I'd say."

I gave Renz a glance. I wouldn't have pictured somebody that young as a ruthless cold-blooded killer, but I'd been wrong before. I jotted that down as Ray continued.

"He had dirty-blond hair that was about an inch long all over his head."

"Like a buzz cut?" Renz asked.

"Yeah, like that, but not as short, and he was taller than you." Ray stared at Renz. "And he looked strong.

"He looked strong how? Wasn't he wearing a coat?" I asked.

"Yep, but everything fit him just right. I could tell he worked out."

"So not overweight, just physically fit?"

"Uh-huh, physically fit. That's one reason I made sure he didn't see me."

"Did he look threatening, like somebody who was capable of intimidating or even punching you if you asked him why he was there?"

"Yep, so I kept my distance. He strutted in, walked to the place where you were standing just before, Agent Jade, looked at the camp, and then headed to the alley like he had a reason to go in there."

"Maybe he was just cutting through," Renz said.

"Nope, because he came back out the same way he went in."

The waitress brought over Ray's plate and set it in front of him. His eyes widened, and that missing-tooth grin lit up his face again. He pulled at my heartstrings, and I remembered my dad telling me years back that I was too much of a softie and people would take advantage of me. Since that day, I'd been cautious and only showed my soft side to people I trusted and the ones who deserved to see it.

"Let's take a break and let Ray enjoy his meal." I topped off all our cups with piping-hot coffee and asked for more sugar packs for Ray.

Chapter 9

I knew we couldn't spend too much time with Ray. That bank camera could very well have caught the image of the person Ray described, and although we had no idea if that man was at all involved in the murder or just happened to pass by, that particular area didn't have any stores or places of interest to be heading to. The timing, if nothing else, was still odd enough for us to question why he was there.

Ray finished his meal and thanked Renz, then we continued the questioning.

"What was the young man wearing, Ray?" I asked.

"Well, I don't know exactly what they're called—stretch pants, maybe? You know, those pants that guys wear these days, the ones that are skintight all the way to the ankles." He shook his head. "Way too pansy ass for my liking. What happened to men looking like men? Did you know that some guys even wear makeup? I mean, what the hell?"

I smiled and continued on. "What color were the pants? And then what was his shirt like if you could see it under the jacket."

Ray waved away my question. "His pants were army

green, and I couldn't see his shirt. He wore a black jeans jacket and black leather combat boots."

"Really?"

Ray nodded. "I may get high on occasion, but my memory is like a steel trap."

"Good to know," Renz said. "Were you close enough to make out any facial features?"

"Nah, like I said, that kid could have wiped the floor with me. I wasn't about to press my luck."

I looked at Renz. "I think we should head back to the camp, drop off Ray, then check out that bank camera and look for a few others. Maybe we'll get lucky and see him on footage somewhere in the area." I turned to Ray. "You still have my card, right?"

"Yes, ma'am, and if I see him again, I'll call you."

"Good. One last question. Did you see which way he went, and did he get into a car?"

"He walked south and then turned right at the next block. That's where I lost sight of him."

Back at the underpass, we thanked Ray, and I watched as he returned to his tent. He looked back, grinned, and waved as we pulled away.

"Fond of the guy, aren't you?" Renz asked.

"Like you aren't?"

"It does feel good to be a decent person now and then."

I laughed. "You're always a decent person, Agent DeLeon. Now let's locate that kid, haul him in for questioning, and find out who he is and why he was there."

Renz drove a block south, a block west, then straight

north to get beyond the freeway and onto Hemmer Street, where the bank was located. He lowered his head and peered out my side of the windshield. "I think that's the building right there. It was white concrete with black-framed windows."

"And it is a bank with storefronts alongside it. Let's go ask some questions."

"Hang on. I think we should call Taft first and tell her we aren't going to make it out to the second location because we're following up on a viable lead here. She can assign someone else to check for cameras in that area."

"Okay, good idea." I absentmindedly stared out the windshield while Renz made the call. Seconds later, as I looked up and down the street at nothing in particular, my body stiffened when I realized the guy Ray had described was standing on the street corner a half block away. I grabbed the door handle, cursed, and leapt out. "He's right there, Renz! Come on!"

Renz ended the call and waved me on as he jumped out of the car, fished change out of his pocket, and fed the meter. He caught up to me and looked around. "Where is he?"

I remained a half block back as I tried to blend in with people on the sidewalk. "He just crossed the street ahead of us. I've got my eyes on him, but what are we supposed to do now, and what has he been up to for the last hour and a half?"

"Good question. Let's follow him for another few minutes while I think of a good reason to approach him. We don't need him running."

"How about I get ahead of him and then walk toward him while you squeeze him in from behind. We have every right to question a person who was at the scene of a murder for no good reason."

"Yeah, you're right. Okay, cross the street, pick up your pace, and get a block ahead of him. Cross over to our side at the next set of lights."

"On it." I checked for cars before bolting across the street and speed walking ahead. I passed the guy within a few minutes and continued on, and occasionally, I would casually stop and glance back to see if Renz was still in my view. He was.

I just need to get beyond the next set of lights, and then I'll cross the street and cut back. Renz has to pick up his pace so we reach the guy at the same time.

I waited at the next set of lights for the crosswalk character to light up and count down the seconds as I crossed. I made a right on the sidewalk and walked toward the man. He was a half block away and heading toward me. Renz needed to speed up. The guy would reach me, pass me, and we would be back in the same boat as before. I stopped and acted like I was window shopping. That would slow down my point of contact with the man while Renz caught up.

It was time to act. The kid was only thirty feet from me, and Renz was twenty feet behind him. I would be the one to make contact with him since, as a woman, I didn't come across as threatening. I stepped away from the store window and into the center of the sidewalk. There was no doubt that the young man matched Ray's description right down to the black combat boots.

"Excuse me. I'm wondering if you can point me in the direction of the army surplus store. I know it's around here somewhere."

"Yeah, I don't know."

He tried to get around me, but I stepped in front of him just as Renz reached his back. We both pulled out our FBI ID's and stuck them in his face.

"We need a word with you," Renz said, "but if you make a scene or try to run, we'll have no choice but to arrest you."

"What the hell are you talking about? Now it's illegal to walk down the sidewalk? I want an attorney."

I chuckled. "For what? You aren't under arrest yet. Now let's go back to our car and have a talk."

"I'm not going anywhere with you." He jerked out of my grip, but Renz was there to grab him.

"Trying to flee from an FBI agent is grounds for arrest. Turn around and put your hands behind your back."

The kid yelled out to get attention. It was obvious from his behavior that he knew exactly what to do. Cell phones came out within seconds, and people followed us as we walked several blocks to the car with a yelling, flailing young man. I rolled my eyes at his foolishness. All he had to do was cooperate, but instead, he felt the need to make a scene and have a tantrum.

We finally made it to the cruiser, where a unit was waiting. I had already called for a police transport to meet us since our car wasn't equipped with a cage or back doors that he couldn't escape from. Transporting the kid in a secured vehicle and talking to him at the police station was safer for everyone, and we needed the interview recorded anyway.

We followed the squad car back to the downtown precinct, only six blocks away, where we were shown to the interview room where the officer had taken the kid. At that point, we hadn't even learned his name. Renz held open the door as I entered then closed it at his back. We both took seats across from our detainee.

"Now, do you want to cooperate or spend the night in jail because you wouldn't answer a few simple questions?"

"You wouldn't tell me why you wanted to question me," he sneered.

"Maybe if you'd given us a minute of your time, you would have found that out," I said. "We need to see your ID."

"Why?"

"Because we want to know who we're talking to." I reached across the table. "ID or a jail cell, your choice." He lifted his hip, pulled out his wallet, and slid it across the table. I pushed it back. "Remove your ID from the plastic sleeve and pass it here."

He cursed but complied. "When are you going to read me my rights?"

Renz took his turn. "Like Agent Monroe said before, you aren't read your rights unless you're under arrest, and we haven't arrested you yet. If you really want your rights read to you—well, you know what comes next." Renz cocked his head. "Your call"—he looked at the ID— "Brandon Dalton."

"Just tell me what you want so I can go about my day."

"Yeah, we could have done that a half hour ago on the sidewalk, but you chose to be belligerent instead." Renz leaned back in the chair. "I'm feeling like a snack right now. How about you, Agent Monroe?"

"Sounds like a great idea. We'll be back soon, Brandon, so just relax and enjoy yourself." I turned and stuck out my hand. "Cell phone."

He gave me the finger before sliding his phone across the table. "You people suck."

"Thanks." I grinned. "Go ahead and stew for a while. We'll be back when we feel like it."

Renz and I walked out and into the next room, where we watched through the one-way glass and listened to him curse for a few minutes.

"Feel like a soda and chips?"

"Yeah, sure."

"Okay, I'll go find a vending machine."

I tipped my wrist when Renz walked out—5:17. A bag of chips would have to do until later. I didn't see myself heading home until eight o'clock at best.

Five minutes later, the sound of a shoe tapping against the door told me Renz was back. I assumed he couldn't open it with two sodas and snacks. I got up and pulled the door inward.

"Thanks."

"You bet." I took one of the sodas and a bag of chips and sat down.

"He saying much to himself?"

"Nah, not really. Mostly cussing us out. Seems like an entitled punk to me, but let's see what the police officer can pull from the database. Maybe he has a record, and maybe he doesn't."

Renz took a seat next to me. "Ray wasn't too far off on the kid's description. Twenty and well built, just like he said."

"And the clothes are a perfect match."

We sat back, enjoyed our sodas and chips, and watched Brandon until it looked like he was bored enough to talk. I doubted that he wanted to sit there all night.

I stretched then stood up. "Ready?"

"Yep. The funny thing is the kid doesn't even know what we want to talk to him about, yet he put up a fight anyway."

I shook my head. "You know what that means, right?"

"Sure do. He's already guilty of something."

We were about to leave when the officer walked in with a sheet of paper in hand.

"Uh-oh," Renz said.

"Yep, he has a police jacket, and believe it or not, his offenses began at age fourteen. All of his juvenile crimes were dismissed with fines and community service, but when he reached eighteen, and then again at twenty, he was charged with battery and served three months and then six months in jail."

"What were the cases?" I asked.

The officer read from the page. "The first offense was

for beating his girlfriend and putting her in the hospital. It looks like she refused to press charges, so the parents did. Apparently, the daughter was a minor. Brandon served three months at the Waukesha County jail and three hundred hours of community service for that one."

Renz tipped his head. "And the second offense?"

The officer frowned. "This guy must have real anger issues. Looks like an unprovoked attack on an elderly woman who was walking her dog. Broke the woman's glasses, two ribs, and she had stitches in her head. Looks like the attack was caught on a store camera, but it took a month to track him down. Meanwhile, the woman moved to Nebraska to live with her daughter."

"Wow, a real Boy Scout," I said.

We thanked the officer. He left the sheet with us and walked out.

I stepped into the hallway. "Let's see what Brandon has to say for himself about this afternoon."

Chapter 10

We returned to the interview room where Brandon sat. He looked up as we entered, gave us his best glare, then huffed.

"It's about damn time. You think I have all night to sit in this hellhole?"

I took a seat. "You have somewhere more exciting to be? Say back at the overpass where you were earlier today?"

"What the hell are you talking about?"

It was time to pull out our "white lie to get the ball rolling" card. Because of Ray's statement, we knew Brandon was there, but we hadn't actually seen him on camera footage yet.

"We saw you on the bank's outdoor camera system that happens to face the freeway's over- and underpass. We had a clear view of you standing between the tent city and the alley off to the west. You seemed to be looking around for something maybe? After that, you entered the alley, were in there for a few minutes, and then came back out. You headed south and then disappeared from the camera view after turning right onto a side street."

"Wow, you have me all figured out. First, it's illegal to

walk down the sidewalk, and then I find out it's also illegal to walk anywhere in the city."

"So you admit you were there? It'd be tough to refute surveillance footage that shows everything about you right down to those combat boots you're wearing."

"Yeah, so what?"

Renz took over. "Why were you there? I wouldn't consider a tent city where drug- and alcohol-addicted homeless people live as being on anyone's bucket list of places to visit."

"I wasn't hanging out there. I was cutting through."

I smiled. "See, that doesn't jibe. If you were cutting through from who knows where, you would have kept going, but you didn't. You wandered around, went into the alley, came back out, and left the way you came. Then an hour and a half later, we find you roaming the sidewalk on an entirely different street in a different direction than where you came from."

Renz played the stare-down game with Brandon. "Where *did* you come from, and how did you get downtown?"

"I took the city bus. Is that a crime too?"

"Nope, not at all, but you still haven't answered our question."

"Yeah, with all your yammering, I forgot what the question was."

"Why were you at the tent city?"

"I wanted to see what a homeless camp looked like. Big deal."

"You mean you wanted to see what a homeless camp

looked like during the daylight hours? Did you drop something there the night before, or thought you did, and went back to have a look?"

"Huh?" He laughed. "You people make no sense."

It was my turn to laugh, and I would be sure to watch his expression closely. "It seems that the same camera caught a crime being committed the night before—say around two a.m. give or take a few minutes."

"Sorry, I can't help you. If I recall, there wasn't much of a moon last night. It had to be darker than hell under that overpass."

"We didn't say the crime was committed under the overpass." Bingo, I had him. Brandon's face went five shades whiter in an instant. "Something wrong, Brandon? It looks like you're about to puke."

He regained his composure, and I assumed he'd been in an interrogation room numerous times before. He was versed in the correct thing to say under pressure. "Show me proof that I was there the night before. Either arrest me—which I'm sure you won't since I've committed no crime—or I'm walking out."

There wasn't anything we could do other than putting him there earlier in the day—and being there earlier in the day wasn't a crime. We had to cut him loose. Forensics needed to process the scene, print everything in the alley, and do a foot search of the area to look for anything on the ground that the police might have missed. We didn't know what we were looking for, but chances were if it was lying there and one of the homeless people saw it, they would have snatched it up and kept it.

We released Brandon to the streets with intentions of digging deeper into his habits, where he currently lived, and what he was using for transportation. People like him were more transient than we were used to. An ID card with a home address and a vehicle registration in the DMV database meant nothing if his plan was to stay off our radar. Until we had more, we couldn't build a case against him.

It was pushing seven o'clock by the time we were back in our car. Renz called Taft to see if any of the agents were going to return to the office that night. She said we would review everything in the morning after Dave updated her on the autopsies with a more accurate time of death for all five victims.

Renz drove us to the office, and we parted ways, each in our personal car. I was exhausted and still had a forty-five-minute drive home. All I wanted was a hot meal, a shower, and a warm bed to climb into.

I called Amber as I drove. "Hey, Sis, what's for supper?"

"You mean the supper we had an hour and a half ago?"

I chuckled. "Yeah, that supper. I'm starving and haven't had anything but a bag of chips since our fast-food lunch earlier today."

"Well, I can easily heat everything up. When will you be home?"

I glanced at the time on the dash. "In forty minutes."

"Good. Expect a couple pieces of fried chicken, mashed potatoes and gravy, and canned corn."

My stomach growled from the description, and I

couldn't wait to dig into that chicken. "Sounds delicious, and I'll see you soon."

As I drove, I thought about Brandon and how we would prove he had a connection to Jane Doe's murder, if he actually did. Forensics was already at the scene, according to the text Renz had sent me minutes earlier, and if lucky, they might find Brandon's prints somewhere on the dumpsters. Yet as damning as that seemed, it didn't put a knife in his hand or give us an eyewitness account of him committing the crime. We had a long way to go with nobody else on our radar as a suspect—and that was just one of the five murders we were dealing with.

I pulled into the garage at twenty after eight. I couldn't believe what I'd thought would be a relaxing Saturday in front of the boob tube while bingeing on made-for-TV movies had turned into a twelve-hour workday.

Inside the house, I found Amber and Kate doing exactly what I was thinking about five minutes prior—bingeing on TV movies, each with a beer and sharing a bowl of extra buttery popcorn.

I dragged myself through the door and leaned against the framework as I stared at them.

Amber paused the TV. "What?"

"You guys have life by the ass."

Kate laughed. "Says the girl who thought working in one county was too restrictive. She needed to get out there, solve crimes across the country, and fly around in an FBI-owned jet like a celebrity. And now with your latest promotion, you're gone even more." She elbowed Amber. "But now, when you have one local case to solve, you're whining about us having it made."

Amber pointed a thumb at Kate. "Yeah, what she said."

I laughed. They made their point and were absolutely right. I was hungry and cranky. "Hey, what's the word for hungry and cranky?"

"Jade?"

"No, I mean the combination of the words."

Kate contorted her face. "Hunky?"

We laughed.

"I need to sit my ass down. Where's that damn chicken?"

Amber joined me in the kitchen and pointed at the table. "Then sit. I'll warm your plate in the microwave. Want a beer?"

"Sure, thanks, Sis."

Seconds later, with a beer and a plate of hot food in front of me, I dug in, and Amber returned to her movie and popcorn.

"Hey, just so you know."

I heard Amber's groan as she paused the TV again. "What?"

"I love you guys."

Kate chuckled. "And we love you too. Now leave us the hell alone so we can watch this movie."

I ate my meal, said good night, and headed to the shower. In twenty minutes, I would be in bed and drifting off to sleep, and I couldn't wait.

Chapter 11

A meeting between Jacob, Evelyn, and their followers began at seven o'clock on Sunday morning. Names had been chosen and tasks assigned for each recruit based on their ambition and ability.

Brandon had been designated to take care of the riskiest task, but with the new development that had been forwarded to Jacob, it looked like Brandon had to be eliminated. There wasn't room in the plans for anyone to go off on their own, do what they wanted, and end up in police custody. There was no excuse for taking that risk, and now, they would be one recruit short.

The recruit who Evelyn had thought would be her pride and joy had failed them miserably, and the consequences would be severe. She and Jacob had spoken with Brandon's handler, who was the person who had seen Brandon being escorted to a police car the day prior and alerted Jacob. Erik Smalley would have to deal with the fallout and personally perform the tasks that Brandon would have been assigned.

Envelopes had been prepared for the meeting and contained sheets of paper listing the name of each victim, their address, their manner of death, and the time the deed was to be done. Each task was outlined in precise detail and set to take place later that night. Brandon would get his envelope just like the others so as not to raise suspicion, but Erik would also get those same instructions. After the meeting, he would take care of Brandon then complete what would have been Brandon's task later that night.

"Any questions?" Jacob asked after instructing Erik on his role and duties.

"No questions, sir. I'm just glad we're going to nip this in the bud before it goes any further. I have no idea why Brandon went back to the underpass, but it was a reckless move on his part. Luckily, after I spotted him, I followed him to Hemmer Street where I saw two plainclothes cops escort him to a squad car. What went on behind closed doors at the police station is anyone's guess, but now he's too much of a risk to continue on. The cops might be following him wherever he goes."

Evelyn looked startled. "What the hell? They better not be following him, or they'll find all of us in here."

"I scanned the area before coming in, ma'am, and didn't see anyone other than the typical vagrants who are always outside."

Jacob nodded. "Okay, okay, let's get this meeting over with and go our separate ways. I want to be notified as soon as Brandon is no longer a threat."

"Roger that, sir."

The meeting began, and just as before, a basket of envelopes was passed to the recruits. Each envelope had a name on it, and the recruit took the corresponding one.

"All the details and instructions are laid out on the paperwork inside. Follow the instructions to the letter, don't improvise a single detail, and you'll be fine. We'll meet back here tomorrow night to hear your reports and to give updates. The grand finale will take place soon."

With the meeting out of the way and each recruit with their instructions, Jacob gave Erik a subtle nod, and everyone dispersed.

As the group walked out, Jacob overheard Erik suggesting that he and Brandon go have breakfast together.

Chapter 12

We gathered in the conference room at eight thirty, each with a cup of coffee in front of us and the half-full carafe centered on the table. Taft was kind enough to bring in two dozen assorted doughnuts, I imagined to compensate us for working through the entire weekend.

Lying at Maureen's left was a folder that more than likely contained the autopsy reports for each of the five victims. The manner of death would be identical for all of them. That, we already knew. The time of death was what we needed to narrow down, and hopefully, Dave had been able to do just that.

"Good morning, Agents." Taft gave us a courtesy nod. "Help yourselves to the doughnuts, and then we'll get the ball rolling. Before we go over the reports that Dave and his team provided me, let's hear any updates that may be of value from when you went back to the crime scenes."

Renz told the group about our encounter with Brandon Dalton and said that while it took us time to question the man and we'd gotten a suspicious vibe from him, we had nothing to charge him with. Kyle and Charlotte had been tasked to our second location, the vacant lot, since we were involved with Brandon at the time. Kyle said they'd watched the gas station videos from last night, but none of the cameras caught that piece of land, and the surrounding buildings blocked what might have been a view anyway. They'd seen people on the sidewalk pass by the cameras, but the darkness and distance made it impossible to tell whether they were looking at men or women. No one else had anything to add.

Taft's expression showed her disappointment. "Okay, then we'll move on to the medical examiner's findings. Dave and his team were kind enough to work through the night so we'd have the results in time for this meeting." She waited while the guys chose a second doughnut and placed them on their paper plates. Once they were settled, she continued. "I've already reviewed these reports, so I'll just pass along the information that's relevant in establishing a perpetrator or several of them. First, every wound appeared to be caused by the same, if not the identical, type of knife. Every point of entry was on the victim's left side of the throat and sliced to the right, meaning the killer was right-handed. That also means the killer was at the victim's rear, pulled their head back, and inflicted the fatal wound. That leads me to believe the attacker either subdued the victim in advance or sneaked up behind them." She glanced down at the papers and sighed. "Okay, so the manner of death, the left-to-right injury, and the weapon of choice is identical for each victim. Now, moving on to the time of death. We've already established the location where each body was found, and from farthest point to farthest point across the city, we have a fifteen-mile drive. That's a significant distance considering it appears that each victim was a convenience kill and not a targeted hit. The killer, or killers, had to be in position at a homeless camp, choose their victim, and then commit the crime. It would seem like an overwhelming task for less than three people since we already know that two of the victims were killed within minutes of each other around the two a.m. hour."

I felt like we should be taking notes, but I knew Taft had already printed out copies of the reports for all of us. All we needed to do was listen.

She continued. "The absolute tightest time frame Dave could give me by the degree of rigor and a more precise body temperature for each victim was that death occurred between one and three a.m. So again, that would be pretty ambitious for two killers. I'm sure we're dealing with three perps, possibly more, and a well-coordinated and planned attack. The question, and the one we're all likely thinking, is why?" Taft opened the floor for a brainstorming session.

I began with what we'd experienced most often in the past—the mindset that homeless people and prostitutes were dispensable. Law enforcement frequently looked the other way simply because family members weren't pressing for answers or a conviction. Oftentimes, family didn't know about the incident, there was no way to contact them, or those same family members had already severed ties with the victim. Also, in many cases, the victim was an unknown, without an ID or fingerprints on record. "So either the killers were out for a joyride to kill for the sake of killing, there was a coordinated attack as Maureen suggested, but that seems like too much planning to just go after homeless people if they were looking for shock value, or—"

Tommy took over. "Or it was only a practice session for something bigger."

Renz squeezed his temples then groaned. "I have to agree with Tommy. Those attacks weren't about the homeless people at all. I think they were being used as guinea pigs."

Kyle pulled back. "For what purpose?"

"To see if the killers had the balls to carry out the plan. To see if that particular method of murder was a good one, and to see if they could get the timing right. Something bigger is going down soon, and as of right now, we have absolutely no idea what that 'bigger' event is going to be."

"Are there any dignitaries coming to town?" Fay asked.

Maureen jabbed the air and pointed at all of us. "Good question, and now would be a great time to start taking notes. Mike, get ahold of the mayor's office and find out if anyone important is coming to Milwaukee in the next week or so. Carl, see if any banks have big money transfers coming up. Charlotte, find out if high-profile convicts are being moved. Kyle, I want you to check into jewelry or high-end art coming into or leaving the city." She swirled her finger. "Yada, yada, yada—you get the point. Start racking your brains and come up with the answer as to why somebody would plan a precisely timed attack and on whom."

We filed out of the conference room with plenty of tasks

to do and questions to answer. It was beginning to look like a far more nefarious plan could be shaping up, and it had nothing to do with homeless people. The lead from Ray was helpful, but the questions we'd posed to Brandon Dalton had gotten us nowhere. He'd claimed that he had the freedom to walk around anywhere he liked, which was true, and we had to release him. Something about the kid stuck in my craw, and besides his narcissistic arrogance and criminal anger issues, he had an attitude that was deeper and much darker. I felt it in my gut and knew we needed to find out more about him.

Back at my desk, I pulled my phone closer and pressed the button for the forensic department. We needed that update about the prints possibly belonging to Brandon and whether anything of evidentiary value was found in the tent city area.

"Forensics, Leah speaking."

"Leah, it's Agent Monroe. Do you have the results back from the investigation at the overpass tent city murder?"

"Yes, but we didn't get anything of value. Several dozen prints were loaded into IAFIS, and there weren't any matches. I imagine most belonged to the homeless people living there. They dumpster dive on a regular basis, you know. The partials we dusted weren't viable either. They were smudged or overlapped other prints."

"Damn it. What about unusual findings on the ground, as if somebody accidentally dropped something that could have been important to them?"

"Sorry, Agent Monroe, but eighteen hours later, if

something was there, a resident from the camp probably snatched it up."

"Yeah, wishful thinking on my part. Okay, thanks."

"You bet."

I groaned in frustration as I placed the receiver back on the base.

"No luck?"

"Nope. Are five homeless people really dead ends?"

"Literally, yes, since we've concluded that the murders probably weren't about them."

"So their murders aren't important?"

Renz frowned. "Of course they are, Jade, but in the dark, seedy world of living on the streets, murders happen often, and unfortunately, people grow numb to it."

I shook my head. "That's unacceptable."

"Then what do you suggest? We have no suspects, witnesses, or reasons why those people were killed. We've already established that the murders weren't about stealing from the homeless, taking their drugs or their cigarettes. It goes way beyond that. Between us and local law enforcement, we need to figure out the bigger picture. When we do, we'll have the murderers, and they'll be held accountable."

I blew out a long breath. "Yeah, I know, but it makes me worry about people like Mary and Ray."

"I hear you, and it's sad to admit that there's thousands of Marys and Rays scattered across the country."

Minutes later, Renz's phone rang. From what I could gather from his end of the conversation, he was talking to Taft. After scribbling something down in his notepad, he hung up and jerked his chin toward the door. "Since we weren't given a task to work on, Taft wants us to join a police unit sitting at a scene on the south side. A delivery truck had a hard time getting through the alley because a car was illegally parked in the driving lane. The driver, already pissed off, banged on the door of the car after honking continuously with no response. He realized then that the man inside the car was either unconscious or dead. The alley isn't far from a homeless camp, and Taft wants our eyes on it to see if we think there could be a connection."

I grabbed my stuff. "Any noticeable injuries?"

"Car doors are locked and the officers couldn't tell, but Taft wants us to take a look anyway."

Chapter 13

The location was fifteen minutes northwest of our office. A small cluster of homes—post-World War II, when the building boom took place—sat on a stark street of cookie-cutter houses. Most were of the two-bedroom one-bath variety and a thousand square feet at most. Alleys ran behind each street of homes, and most of them had garage access.

Renz turned in to the alley behind Miller Street, where the car and man were supposedly located.

I pointed halfway down the block. "Right there. The lights are still flashing on the squad car."

Renz parked in a visitors' space, and the slab of concrete wedged between houses could accommodate up to four cars. We climbed out and crossed the alley to the squad car. A fifty-foot area of yellow tape temporarily surrounded the vehicle in question. When we approached, both squad car doors opened, and the officers stepped out. Renz made the introductions, and we asked for details as we followed them to the car.

After peering in the window and banging on the glass,

all I could determine was that the occupant looked like a sleeping man. His head was slumped against his chest, and he didn't move a muscle when I yelled out. "You think he's dead? Maybe he's sleeping off an all-night drinking binge."

"All we know is what the delivery truck driver said when he called 911."

"And that was?" Renz asked.

"That an unconscious or dead man was in a car in this alley. We spoke to the delivery truck driver for a few minutes, got his contact info, and reported our findings. I guess because the 911 report came in as a possible deceased person in a vehicle, and at that particular location, it triggered a call to your FBI supervisor."

Renz gave the officer the go-ahead to break the passenger-side window so we could get in and figure out if the man was dead or just unconscious. We gloved up and stepped aside while the officer came forward with his glass breaker. With a hard thrust, he shattered the safety glass, and it spiderwebbed and buckled. Renz pulled it to the ground, unlocked the door, and climbed inside.

"Okay, let's see what we have. Hey, buddy, you alive?"

I watched as Renz reached in and shook the unresponsive man by the shoulder then lifted his head.

"Shit! This isn't good, Jade. Call Taft and tell her we need Forensics and Dave out here right away. This guy isn't just stone-cold dead. He's also Brandon Dalton." Renz backed out of the car. "We have to leave things as they are until they get here. I don't want to contaminate the scene." He looked at the officers. "Meanwhile, let's cordon off a hundred feet in each direction."

A dozen scenarios passed through my mind as we waited. There was no way that Brandon's death was a coincidence—the timing was too perfect. "Renz, if he was murdered, then that means somebody besides us was following him yesterday. They must have seen us with him and then watched as the police unit hauled him away."

Renz kicked an empty soda can across the alley. It bounced into the bushes along a garage, where a cat sprang out, hissed, and disappeared around the corner. "Yeah, I was thinking along those lines, too, but then did that person kill him? If so, then they had to know each other."

I approached the officer whose name tag had M. Knox on it. "Did either of you call in this car's tag number?"

Knox said he had and that it was registered to an Elias Kotar, who'd reported it stolen three days prior.

I groaned. "Of course it was. Why can't we catch a damn break?"

Renz frowned. "I thought we had a chance with Brandon being a real lead. Another day of digging into his background and what he was up to could have given us something to hold him on."

I glanced at the car. "And he wouldn't be sitting in there dead right now."

Dave and the forensic team arrived a few minutes later and took up the rest of the visitor spots.

"What have we got other than the obvious reason I'm here?" Dave slid off the van's seat and to the ground.

Leah Jasper and Terry Franklin, the county's weekend

forensic techs, were right behind him with their testing kits and camera.

"Dead man behind the wheel. He just happens to be somebody we questioned yesterday about the five homeless killings."

Dave shook his head. "When it rains, it pours."

I had to agree. We moved aside so the forensic techs could do their job before Dave took over the scene.

Leah busied herself with the camera while Terry dusted the door handles, steering wheel, seat belt latches, dash, trunk latch, and every surface that a hand or fingers might have touched.

"Uh, guys, did you see this?" Leah backed out of the car and waved us over.

"What have you got?" I asked.

"The back of the driver's seat has a gunshot hole in it. There's gunpowder residue in a three-inch circle around it. I imagine once you lift the body out, you'll see a kill shot to his back and a very bloody seat behind him."

"Damn it." Renz rounded the car with me on his heels. He peered into the open rear door and looked at the obvious hole in the back of the driver's seat. He backed out, let me take a look, then rubbed his forehead as we contemplated the scenario that might have taken place. "So, somebody either lay in wait inside the car and forced Brandon to drive here, or Brandon and whoever killed him were going somewhere together, ended up here, and then the other person used a ruse to climb into the back seat, possibly to get something, then shot Brandon."

I let out an anxious breath. "We could make the scenario fit any narrative we want. What all of this is telling me, though, is that Brandon was involved in the killings and somebody took him out to keep him quiet."

Renz called out to Dave. "We need a rough estimate on how long he's been dead." He turned to the officers. "When did the 911 call come in?"

Knox walked to his car, checked with the 911 dispatch, then crossed back to us. "The call was recorded at exactly eight twenty-two this morning. The driver thought he called around eight fifteen, but it's always best to get the exact time from the 911 operator. People often miscalculate times."

I knew that for a fact. People had the worst recall, even if it was just hours after an incident.

Dave climbed into the car and did his initial analysis. He popped his head out a minute later. "This man has been dead less than two hours. Rigor is just starting to take hold, and his body temp is ninety-seven degrees, give or take. Of course, that's speculative since it's a field exam."

I glanced at my watch—9:57. "So likely between seven thirty and eight thirty?"

"Sounds probable." Dave called out to his assistant, Tyler, to bring over the gurney and a body bag. "Once we lift him out, we'll be able to see the extent of his injury. Since there isn't an exit wound, I'd venture to say the projectile is lodged in his body and likely tore up numerous organs and his rib cage."

I grimaced at the thought, shielded my eyes, and did a

three sixty of the alley. It was obviously daylight when Brandon was shot, a risky move in a residential neighborhood, but since it was a Sunday and early morning, there was less of a chance of being seen. I was hoping to see a camera somewhere but didn't. "Do you think the seat and the cushioning it provided acted as a silencer of sorts?"

Leah fielded that question. "A thick foam cushion will indeed buffer the sound of a gunshot, so not only was the victim taken by surprise, but the blast was muffled too. The perp probably walked away within seconds, and nobody was the wiser."

"That's how I see it going down," Renz said.

Dave tipped his head at Tyler then at us. "Ready to get him out?"

"Go ahead and lift him forward so Leah can snap a few pics of his back and the seat before you remove him from the car."

Dave pulled Brandon forward, and Leah took a half dozen pictures. She nodded when she had enough. Brandon was lifted out of the car, turned onto his side on the gurney for observation and more pictures, then placed flat in the body bag. Dave zipped it up. "We'll get him back to the office, clean him up, and try to retrieve that bullet."

I turned to Leah. "We're going to need your garage's flatbed out here to pick up the car."

"Sure, I'll call for it now."

Chapter 14

It was noon by the time we'd returned to our office. Renz had updated Taft every half hour, Brandon's body was taken to the medical examiner's office, and the car was in the county crime lab's garage and being processed from top to bottom.

We gathered again in the conference room, where everyone had a few minutes to report on the jobs they were assigned that morning. The mayor's office didn't know of any dignitaries coming to town for personal, political, or educational reasons. The art museum had nothing extraordinary on loan coming in or going out, and the jewelry stores didn't have unusual amounts of diamonds being shipped in from Antwerp. Neither the casino nor any city banks were moving large sums of money, but worst of all, we didn't know who killed Brandon.

I tapped my pen as I thought and then presented my idea. "What if we go back to where we caught sight of Brandon yesterday, check every store that has a camera, and see if we catch him or ourselves on the footage. If someone was following him before we were, we'd notice them following us, too, once he was in our custody."

"Not a bad idea," Renz said.

Maureen closed the folder in front of her. "As long as nobody has any leads to follow through on, I want half of you to contact the police departments in the jurisdictions where the crimes took place, find out if they've heard any local chatter from their confidential informants, and see if they've followed up on the restaurants where there's homeless camps on the sidewalks and if they've spoken with the sanitation departments. Before I completely rule out the targeted killing of homeless people, I want to make sure the police followed through with talking to those sources. Renz, Jade, Kyle, and Charlotte, I want you four to hit every store on that street that has cameras to see if you can spot someone following Brandon and then yourselves." Taft stood. "Let's get busy. I'll check with the sheriff's office to see if they've made any progress, and then I want everyone back here at five o'clock for a wrap-up meeting."

We headed out knowing full well that at least half the stores would be closed because it was Sunday, but we would do our best with the ones that were open and hope they had cameras facing the street. Unfortunately, we didn't know where Brandon had spent that hour and a half between the time he left the underpass tent city and when I spotted him on the sidewalk. The only way to tell if he was being followed was if the same person was spotted behind him and then again behind us. If we did see someone, our tech department could use the facial-recognition software to see if there was a match in the criminal database.

"Too bad it's Sunday," I said and then waited for someone to ask why. Finally, Charlotte did.

"Okay, why is it too bad it's Sunday other than the obvious reason we'd said earlier about stores being closed?"

"Because the bank is closed, too, and they would definitely have cameras outside, especially in front of the building where the armored trucks park."

"Hmm… that's a fact all right," Kyle said. "They'd also have the best equipment, meaning we'd see the clearest images."

I added my two cents. "Which would work the best with the facial rec software." I pulled my phone from my pocket. "What was the name of the bank, Renz?"

"Milwaukee First Bank."

"Oh yeah." I tapped the name into the search bar and waited. That name was obviously a branch of banks since five of them popped up in Milwaukee County. I located the one on Hemmer Street and tapped on the website. It showed the days and hours of operation, and as expected, they were closed on Sundays.

Renz called back to me. "What are you doing?"

"Trying to find a number for somebody who will come down here, open the bank, and let us view their footage."

Charlotte sighed. "Good luck with that."

"Well, if you don't try, you'll never succeed."

Renz chuckled from the driver's seat. "I like that about her. She's like a trained sniffing dog, but instead of sniffing for drugs, she sniffs for the bad guy."

"Gotta sniff them out, partner."

"Damn straight. Have you found a number yet?"

"Give me a minute, and I'll let you know. I had success once with finding out who owned a hotel. I called him at home in the middle of the night because his night manager was rude and abrasive to me. He was shocked that I was able to track down his name and home number. Maybe I can do that with the bank president or somebody in an upper tier of management." I continued searching my phone while Renz drove. After exhausting the bank's website for a personal number, I moved on to the "who is" database and entered the name of the bank manager, assuming I would catch her at home easier than I would the bank president. I tapped the name Elizabeth Morrison and Milwaukee into our prepaid account and waited for the results that would give me her age, relatives, phone number, and address. The easy accessibility of that information was scary, yet it was all public record that anyone could access at the courthouse if they had the time and tenacity. This way was faster and easier. "Got it. Now let's see if anyone answers the phone. I don't know if the number they show is her cell or a landline."

"Who are you trying to call?" Kyle asked.

"The bank manager. I figured she might be easier to reach than the bank president." I waited. "Okay, it's ringing."

"Put it on Speakerphone," Renz said.

I did that before someone picked up, then we waited as the phone rang on Elizabeth Morrison's side.

"Hello."

I wasn't actually expecting anyone to answer and was

taken aback but collected myself quickly. "Hello, is this Elizabeth Morrison?"

"Yes it is. May I ask who's calling?"

"Yes, ma'am. This is SSA Jade Monroe from the FBI."

"Is this some kind of a joke?"

"I assure you, ma'am, it isn't. I have you on the line with three other agents, and we need your help."

"You need my help? With what?"

I continued. "Ma'am, we need to access the footage from yesterday on your bank's camera that faces Hemmer Street."

"I'm sorry, but this sounds like a prank. I'm going to hang up."

I held my phone against Renz's right shoulder so he could add his two cents. "Mrs. Morrison, this is Senior Special Agent Lorenzo DeLeon, and I assure you this isn't a prank. If you feel more comfortable about it, we can have a patrol unit pick you up. It's imperative that we see yesterday's footage."

"I'd have to clear it with the bank president first. I can't just waltz in there after hours and do whatever I like. I'd be fired immediately."

"Ma'am, our supervisory agent can take care of all those details. We really don't have time to wait. All she'd need is the president's name and police units can track him down and explain to him as well what's going on."

"What actually *is* going on?"

"It's a life-or-death matter, but because it is an active investigation, we can't tell you anything more than that. Would you like a police escort? I can arrange for a unit to pick you up in five minutes."

"Yes, I suppose, but somebody absolutely needs to contact the bank president, and I'll try to reach him, too, during the drive."

"That's a great idea. I'll have a patrol unit at your door in five minutes." Renz rattled off her address that I'd just written down and read it to her, and she acknowledged that it was correct. "Thank you, ma'am, and we'll meet you in front of the bank in fifteen minutes."

I clicked off the call, contacted Taft, and told her we would be viewing the bank's footage within the hour but said she needed to explain our situation to the bank president. I gave her his name and number, and she said she'd take care of it immediately.

Chapter 15

Renz found street parking nearby, and we walked to the front doors of the bank. Within five minutes, a patrol unit pulled up and double-parked with its lights flashing, and the officers climbed out. Elizabeth Morrison exited the back seat of the squad car and approached us, and with my badge in hand, I introduced her to our group. Kyle asked the officers to stick around the area but said it could be up to an hour before she would be back out.

I assured Elizabeth that Taft, our supervisor, had gotten through to the bank president and explained why we were there.

"It's all fine, and he said he trusts you one hundred percent to help us with the camera footage." I saw what looked like relief spread across her face.

Inside, Elizabeth walked us to the security office, where each camera had its own monitor. There were six in total, but all we needed to see were the two that faced the overpass and Hemmer Street. At that moment, the Hemmer Street footage from yesterday was the most important.

Elizabeth queued up the recording. "What time would

you like it to begin?"

I thought about the time we'd returned to the underpass. "Let's start at three o'clock. We already had our man in question at the downtown precinct by five, so between three and four forty-five is the time frame we need."

"Sure, not a problem, Agent Monroe." Elizabeth set the parameters and let the recording roll.

It took a good ten minutes before we spotted Brandon at the crosswalk. As soon as the light changed, he crossed the street and turned east on Hemmer.

"I wonder what he's up to and where he's been since Ray saw him. Brandon said he took the bus to the area, but from where, and why walk so far? There's a bus stop on every other block."

Kyle nodded. "Let's see if we can figure that out." He pointed at a man we had been watching for a few minutes. He always remained about a hundred feet behind Brandon. Other people entered and exited stores, passed him, crossed to the opposite side of the street, or fell farther back.

"That guy is walking lockstep with Brandon, but every time Brandon looks around, the guy turns his back to him or ducks into a store entryway. He has to be the one following him."

"Let's fast-forward to when we showed up on the scene. We'll have copies of these recordings sent to our office anyway, and we can look at them later in closer detail. What time do you think we arrived and you parked, Renz?"

He checked his phone for the time he had called Taft.

"I was on the phone with Maureen at ten minutes after four, and that's when you bolted out of the car."

"Okay, let's start at four o'clock and see if that guy is still in the area."

Luckily, the bank had two street-facing cameras, and both had wide-angle capabilities. From the bank, we were able to see people three blocks in either direction, although not well enough to identify anyone.

"There he is." Charlotte pointed at a clothing store across the street. That same man was standing in front of it as if debating on going in. "Now, where is Brandon in relation to him?"

"Brandon was on our side of the street and a half block up, just ready to cross at the lights."

The camera showed us parking, and about ninety seconds later, I bolted out of the car and began walking east. Renz was behind me within seconds.

Kyle laughed. "You seriously plugged the meter?"

Renz shrugged. "I didn't want a ticket, and I told you, Monroe is like a tracking dog. I knew she was on top of it."

I chuckled. "Okay, okay, let's focus on the footage. There, the guy is on the move again, but check it out. As soon as I crossed to his side, he stopped and waited until I got ahead of him. He must have noticed that we were following Brandon."

We watched his every movement, and he remained behind me at all times. When I crossed the street ahead of Brandon and started backtracking, the guy stopped and watched from his side of the street.

Kyle scratched his cheek while staring at the screen. "So he isn't moving in because he sees what's about to play out from across the street."

We watched as Renz and I squeezed Brandon in, had verbal exchanges with him, then led him back in the direction we came from. At that point, the guy crossed to our side of the street but remained far enough behind us to go unnoticed. He watched as the squad car pulled up, Brandon was put in the back, and the car pulled away.

Renz let out a long breath and checked the time on the monitor. "Okay, we left the scene at quarter of five."

I turned to Elizabeth. "We're going to need this footage and the footage from the camera that faces the freeway overpass, both from yesterday. You can send the recordings to my email address." I handed her my card. "We really appreciate your help, Mrs. Morrison, and I'm sure our supervisor will call in a personal thank-you to the bank president for your assistance."

She nodded. "I'll get the footage sent over to you right away."

We thanked her, then Renz contacted the police unit, and they returned to the bank to take Elizabeth home.

We were back at the office by three o'clock and excited to get the image of that guy's face to our tech department. If the man had a police record, he would pop up on facial rec, and we'd be able to find out everything we needed to know about him. He was tracking Brandon for a reason, and he was likely Brandon's killer. We had to dig deeper into Brandon's life, inform his family of his death, and find out who the mystery man was as soon as possible.

Once at my desk, I saw that the email had come in. I forwarded the video and the time to start watching it to our tech department. "Want to go with me?" I asked Renz.

"Downstairs to Tech?"

"Yep. We have to point out to them who they need to get the facial rec on, and hopefully, at some point in the video, they can get a straight-on view of him."

"Yeah, sure. Everything kind of depends on identifying him anyway. We'll watch the underpass video later, or I can forward it to one of the other agents to watch."

I swatted the air. "That part of the case is ours to follow. Once we find out who the mystery guy is, everyone can jump on board to apprehend him. Chances are, if there are prints on the car, they might be his."

"Speaking of that, I wonder if Forensics came up with anything."

I opened our office door and tipped my head toward the stairs. "One problem at a time. Taft can delegate who checks into the car and who talks to the owner. We just need to identify that guy."

I always opted for the stairs rather than the elevator if I had a choice. We spent a good amount of time sitting, whether that was at our desks, in a car, or on an airplane, and anytime I could be off my butt, I was happy. I bolted down the stairs and had already given our tech department a heads-up that we were on our way.

That Sunday, Betsy Johansson and Marty Trent were on board. We entered the seventy-degree room, and when I felt the goose bumps rise on my arms, I immediately grabbed a spare lab coat off the wall hook.

"Hey, guys," I said, "you got my video, right?"

Betsy turned toward me. "Yep, and we're at the three o'clock starting point like you suggested. All we need is to see who we're looking for and then freeze the image when we get a good shot of him." She rolled the video, and at the fifteen-minute spot, I pointed out the man who had been following Brandon. "So the guy wearing the blue windbreaker, jeans, and with the ear-length black hair?"

"That's the guy. He stays on that side of the street and only crosses over once Renz and I have Brandon in custody. I recall seeing him look around on several occasions and directly at the bank after we handed off Brandon to the police. I'm sure you'll get a direct face shot of him along the way."

"Good enough. Want me to call you as soon as we find out something?"

"Absolutely, and if I'm not at my desk, try my cell."

Renz and I headed up the stairs and passed Taft's office on the way to ours. That time, she was at her desk when we walked by. She called out to us, and we turned back.

"Just an FYI," she said. "The forensics lab just checked in. The prints they did collect belonged to Brandon Dalton and the car's owner, but none of the other prints found were in the system."

"Why were the owner's prints on file?" Renz asked.

"He's a guard at the women's retention facility in New Berlin. He said that car wasn't his everyday work car, but he and his wife did use it as a spare. Her prints were likely in there, too, but she isn't on record anywhere."

I shook my head. "So the killer was either gloved or doesn't have an arrest record, and that would make the facial rec useless if he and the guy following Brandon are one and the same."

"Unfortunately, that's true. Tech is checking it out?"

"As we speak, and they'll contact us as soon as they know something. We were going to dig deeper into Brandon Dalton, find out where he lives, and contact his next of kin."

"Wasn't there a cell phone on his person?"

"Nope. The killer must have taken it," Renz said.

"Okay, keep me posted."

Back at our desks, we pondered the fastest way to find out where Brandon lived. His driver's license had never been updated after a move a year earlier, and different tenants lived at that location now.

"Okay, no phone and no current address. Tax returns, maybe?"

"We don't have his social security number, and that address might be the same as the one on his driver's license," Renz said.

"Then how do we find his family? Maybe the 'who is' app?"

Renz disagreed. "No, that's for businesspeople, but we could try the people search app."

I frowned. "That information is always so outdated."

"True, but they usually list other people with that same last name who might be related. It's worth a try."

I rolled my chair over to his desk. "Go for it, then."

Renz logged on to the site, typed in Brandon's name with his middle initial, *R*, and waited as the program gathered the results. "Here we go." Renz pointed as one by one, the results popped up.

I sighed. "Same address as what's on his driver's license."

"Right, but there are four other people who could possibly be relatives in Wisconsin." Renz wrinkled his brow and tapped the screen. "Either of these two guys could be his father since the age is right."

"Let's give them a call and find out. Hopefully, those phone numbers are current."

Renz dialed the first number. The name attached to it was a Jeffrey Dalton out of Wisconsin Rapids. A woman with a sweet-sounding voice answered and listened as Renz asked if they were related to a Brandon Dalton from Milwaukee. She said it was a possibility, but since she'd been married to Jeff for only a year, she didn't know his extended family. She said that Jeff didn't have any sons, but he did have two daughters. Renz thanked her and hung up. The second number belonged to a Robert Dalton, which seemed promising since Brandon's middle name was Robert. He was out of Racine, a Lake Michigan city not too far south of Milwaukee. The phone rang four times then went to voicemail. Renz left his name and number and asked for a call back.

"Doubt if the guy is at work on a Sunday, so hopefully, he'll take my message seriously and return my call."

"Set your phone alarm to try again in an hour." I looked

at the other names. One was a woman, Delores, age thirty-four, and the other was a male, Carlton, age thirty-eight, both Milwaukee residents. "Seems like a stretch to think Brandon could possibly have siblings that much older than himself."

"And at forty-seven, that would put Robert out of the age group to be Brandon's father," Renz said.

"Maybe they're older cousins."

"Or no relative at all, but we need to call and find out." Renz tapped the buttons on his desk phone and called Delores first. A female voice answered right away, a positive start. Renz introduced himself and asked if she was related to Brandon Dalton.

"Yeah, his dad and my own were brothers. Why?"

"Were?"

"Brandon's dad died in a car accident two years back, and Brandon has been on his own ever since. The mom skipped town with a coworker more than ten years ago."

"That's a shame. Does Brandon have any siblings?"

"Yes, a sister, Chloe, who is married and lives in Salt Lake City, Utah."

"And Chloe's married name?"

"Um, darn, I can't think. I haven't seen her since she moved away and got married. That was five years ago."

"How about her age, then?"

"She's twenty-seven, I think. Oh, I remember now. Her last name is Hughes."

"Great, so Chloe would be Brandon's only immediate next of kin?"

"That's correct. Nobody ever found out what happened to their mom or where she went. Is something wrong with Brandon? I mean, why would the FBI call me?"

"I'm sorry to inform you that Brandon died this morning, and that's why we're trying to locate his relatives."

"Oh my God, that's terrible. We weren't close since I'm much older than he is, but he was still family. May I ask what happened?"

"It was a car accident," Renz said.

The statement was literally true if somewhat of a white lie. Renz thanked her and ended the call.

"So, should we call the sister now? Maybe she has some insight as to what Brandon has been up to."

Renz shook his head. "We'll call her as a formality so she can arrange to deal with his remains, but as far as her knowing anything about his recent life, I sincerely doubt that she would. She lives fourteen hundred miles away, is seven years older than him, and married. I can't see what they would have in common or what they would even talk about during a phone call."

I agreed with Renz's logic, but the call needed to happen anyway, and there was no time like the present. I did a quick internet search for the name Chloe Hughes in Salt Lake City, and a match popped up with a phone number. I cocked my head at Renz. "Ready?"

"Yep."

I read off the phone number, and he made the call.

Chapter 16

Renz had ended the call with Chloe ten minutes prior. He told me that she sounded devastated, considering that Brandon was her only immediate relative, but admitted they didn't often talk. Chloe said she would handle the burial arrangements as soon as we released his body from our custody.

We waited on pins and needles for word back from the tech department, and at three thirty, my desk phone finally rang.

"This is either going to be good news or bad." I reached for the receiver.

Renz chuckled. "Well, yeah, fifty-fifty odds of either one."

I flipped him the bird and answered the phone. "Agent Monroe here."

"Jade, it's Betsy. We have a facial match."

I fist-pumped the air and leapt from my chair. "We'll be right down." I hung up. "Yes! They have a match."

Renz and I bolted from our office and headed for the stairs. We made it to Tech in under two minutes.

I burst through the door with Renz on my heels. "So who is he?" I asked.

Betsy waved us over to her computer screen. "Here's your guy, and his name is Erik Smalley."

"Who the hell is Erik Smalley? He obviously has a criminal record, or he wouldn't be in the system."

"He does, although it isn't anything earth-shattering. He's been arrested four times for unlawful assembly and instigating riots. He seems to be an activist for any issue that may be controversial to mainstream America. He's single, twenty-six, and lives with two other like-minded individuals who previously have been arrested too."

I groaned. "But going from protesting to murder? Seems like quite a leap to me."

Renz agreed. "True, but it's time to pay Mr. Smalley a visit. We'll need that information printed out, Betsy."

"You bet." Seconds later, she had the four-page arrest report, along with Erik Smalley's personal information, printed out. She handed the documents to Renz. "Good luck, guys."

Renz tipped his head toward the door. "Come on. We have to go over this with Taft before anything else."

Back upstairs, we headed down the hall to our supervisor's office. Renz gave Taft's door two raps, and after looking up from her computer, she waved us in.

"What have you got?"

"A positive match." I heard the enthusiasm in my voice as I said the words.

"Really?" Taft gave us her full attention. "Sit down and tell me everything."

Renz explained that although Erik Smalley's police record didn't involve significant crimes, there could be something brewing that he and Brandon were part of. The fact that he'd witnessed Brandon being put into the back seat of a police car might have been enough reason to get the okay to end Brandon's life before he or other people were named.

Taft frowned. "But that makes me wonder, especially if they were working together, why Erik would have been following Brandon to begin with." She tapped her pen against the legal pad to her right. "Brandon had a police jacket, too, correct?"

I took my turn. "Yes, but not for the same type of activity. Brandon was arrested on several occasions for being physically abusive, and Erik's arrests were primarily because of the ruckus he caused while demonstrating and rioting."

"So mix rioting with physical assault and you have a pretty good tag team of dangerous individuals, especially if they're teaming up with more people with the same mindset. The question is why?"

Renz informed Taft that Erik Smalley had two roommates, a Lucas Freeman and a Cole Pratt, also with arrests under their belts for the same type of offenses.

"Okay, haul him in for questioning and take Kyle and Charlotte with you, especially since there may be other people at the residence."

"You got it, Boss."

We made our way northwest to West Allis, a working-class suburb of Milwaukee with older homes and apartments. According to the address on record, Erik lived in an upper apartment of a duplex on the corner of West Greenfield Avenue and South Sixtieth Street, just a stone's throw from the Veteran's Affairs complex.

Renz parked a half block away so we could size up the building without them noticing. We had to consider the fact that if Erik had shot and killed Brandon, then he was an armed and dangerous man with two roommates who could be armed and dangerous too. We had to put eyes on every outer door of that building before ringing the bell. We exited the vehicle and walked to the alley behind the residence. At the back of the house was a fire escape for the second floor. The sides of the house didn't have any doors, so we would have to cover only the front and back exits. Kyle and Charlotte quietly ascended the rear stairs, and we rounded the house, stepped up to the front porch, and Renz rang the buzzer for the second-floor apartment.

Seconds later, we heard someone running down the stairs. Renz gave me that nod, meaning I needed to have my guard up and be ready for anything.

The door swung open widely, without caution, as if whoever answered it was expecting someone. From the look on his face, we weren't the intended guests.

"What the—who the hell are you?"

His expression told us he was about to slam the door, but with Renz's foot already beyond the threshold, the man wouldn't be able to slam it even if he tried.

Renz pushed farther in. "We're the FBI, and we need to speak with Erik Smalley."

"Um—he isn't here."

"Step aside. We'll check for ourselves." With the man backed against the stairs, he had nowhere to go but up. Renz jerked his chin and unholstered his weapon. "Move it."

I had my gun drawn as well. We had no idea if that man was there alone or if more people were in the apartment, but we were about to find out.

A voice called out from above us. "Is it Damon?"

I looked up at the face of Erik Smalley, and he bolted. I knew he wouldn't get far, and as soon as we cleared the stairs, Kyle was pushing him back into the apartment.

Renz yelled out, "Who else is here?"

Erik jerked out of Kyle's grasp. "Nobody, man. What the hell is this?"

Charlotte and I cleared the small apartment in a matter of seconds. "We're good. It's only these two inside."

"Sit your asses down." Kyle looked at the twentysomething kid who'd answered the door. "What's your name?"

"Go to hell. I don't have to say a word to you."

"Okay, you want to play hardball, then you'll both be arrested. Jade, call the West Allis PD and get a unit to this address immediately."

"On it."

"What's with kids these days?" Renz asked. "Is it really that tough to get people to cooperate and answer a few simple questions?"

I huffed. "Apparently so, and we've seen it firsthand in the last twenty-four hours."

Ten minutes later, Charlotte, who was watching the

street from the kitchen window, called out to us in the living room. "The squad car just pulled up."

Renz gestured. "Okay, both of you stand up and put your hands behind your backs. You'll be questioned at the police station, and since you're uncooperative, you'll both be detained for now."

Two officers entered the kitchen, where we had Erik Smalley and, according to the driver's license Renz pulled from the roommate's wallet, Lucas Freeman in custody.

"Throw them in separate interview rooms at your precinct. We'll be right behind you."

The police department was fifty blocks west of the duplex, a fifteen-minute drive without lights flashing and sirens blaring.

Both men were taken in through the garage entrance, as was standard practice at most police stations. We parked in the front lot and entered the building, then Charlotte and I sat while Renz and Kyle walked up to the counter and explained who we were and why we were there.

Moments later, Officer Conrad met us in the lobby and walked us back to the interview rooms. Our focus was on Erik Smalley, and unless Lucas Freeman had outstanding warrants, he would be released.

Renz and I entered interview room one, where Erik sat. Kyle and Charlotte took room two and planned to question Lucas about his relationship with Erik and where they both had been and with whom over the last two days.

We took seats across from Erik, and I placed his police jacket on the table. His eyes darted toward it.

"What's that?"

"Where were you this morning say around eight o'clock?" Renz asked.

"Sleeping."

"Can anyone confirm that?"

Erik shrugged. "Don't know since I was asleep."

I chuckled. "Cute. Why were you following Brandon Dalton and then us yesterday?"

His face went white.

Renz leaned in. "Cat got your tongue? The agent asked you a question."

"I wasn't following anyone. I have no idea what you mean."

"We have you on camera following Brandon and us all the way to the police car. Let me refresh your memory." I opened the folder and slid several still shots across to him.

"There's suddenly a law against walking up and down Hemmer Street?"

"We didn't mention the street name, and there aren't any store names in view. There's no way to identify that street by these photos, Erik. Why was Brandon at the tent city underpass?"

"I don't know what you're talking about, and I don't know of any tent city."

"The homeless people under the overpass. You don't know anything about them when you were following Brandon from there? That's not the story we got from him yesterday when we interviewed him. As a matter of fact, we're having a second interview with him later today. Seems that he has a lot more to tell us."

"That's impossible."

I glanced at Renz then back at Erik. "Why is that?"

He froze for a second then came up with a fast lie. "Because I don't know anyone named Brandon."

"Do you own a firearm, Erik?"

"No."

"So our agents who are tearing apart your apartment as we speak won't find a handgun there?"

He sneered in our faces. "You have a warrant?"

I laughed. "That was issued within minutes. Ever hear of probable cause?"

Erik laughed back. "I want an attorney."

We stood up and walked out.

Chapter 17

We met up with Kyle and Charlotte in the hallway. Kyle was already shaking his head. "Kids are sure different than when I was growing up."

I rolled my eyes. "They sure are. Get anywhere with Lucas?"

"Nope. The PD is checking to see if he has a record or open warrants, but so far, he hasn't told us anything," Kyle said.

I continued. "And Erik is a cocky one. Says he's done talking, not that he's said anything except about being asleep at eight o'clock this morning. Although he did go pale when we showed him the photos from yesterday. I bet he thinks we were bluffing about searching his residence."

Renz shook his head. "Because we were, but now, I'm thinking we actually should. I'll call Taft and get her opinion."

"It would definitely move the case along if we found a gun and the slug matched the one Dave took out of Brandon's body." I frowned. "Yet the comment about searching his place didn't seem to shake him up too much."

Charlotte added her opinion. "Maybe it's somebody else's gun and he's already given it back to them."

"And that's a real possibility." Renz held up his finger after dialing Taft, and we waited as they talked. He ended the call in less than a minute. "Taft said she's going to expedite getting a warrant for that duplex. She also said the projectile removed from Brandon's right lung was from a nine-millimeter bullet."

"The typical choice of handguns these days and plentiful on the street," Kyle said.

"Both guys will stay put until we hear back about the warrant. Taft said she should have an answer within a half hour."

"And if there isn't a gun in the residence, we'll have to release them without any answers whatsoever as to why Erik was following Brandon or even how he knew him."

Renz nodded. "That's true, Jade, and unfortunately, even when our gut tells us one thing, the law says we have to do another. We might not agree or like it, but it is what it is."

"And that's when we do our best to gather as much evidence as possible and build an irrefutable case," Kyle said.

"As long as we have to wait for an answer from Taft, who wants to join me in the cafeteria? I can really use a snack and some coffee."

I smiled at Renz. "Do you get up in the middle of the night to eat?"

"Not yet, but maybe I'll start setting my alarm." He

nudged me. "Come on, guys. We have nothing but time on our hands anyway."

At five thirty, we were sitting in the police station's cafeteria and filling our bellies with sandwiches and chips when Renz's phone rang. Taft had gotten the warrant, and the upper duplex on West Greenfield Avenue was being searched.

"My bet is that they'll find nothing incriminating," Renz said.

I groaned. "I have to agree. Those guys are a bit more savvy than the typical person who teeters on the edge of criminal activity. It's like we said before—there's a bigger picture involved, but they aren't going to admit it exists."

"We'll figure it out, and hopefully, that happens before more people die," Kyle said.

I stared at the wall clock for the next half hour then heard the buzz of Renz's phone. A text had come in.

He pulled it from his pocket, read it, and cursed. "We have to cut them loose. Nothing incriminating was found at the duplex."

"Damn it. How about putting a car on them to see what they do?" I suggested.

Kyle shook his head. "That probable cause ace we had up our sleeve was just used and got us nowhere. If we follow them without a justifiable reason, they can cite harassment. Taft isn't going to okay it. We need to put in the legwork and come up with evidence that puts Brandon, Erik, or Lucas, their fingerprints, or their DNA at one of the murder scenes."

"Yeah, and it would be a foolish move to hold my breath on the chances of that happening since we didn't have any luck with Brandon."

An officer walked in with papers in hand. He took a seat next to us.

I tipped my chin his way. "Got something on Lucas Freeman?"

"Word for word nearly the same arrest record that Erik has. Makes sense that they'd cover for each other."

Renz scanned the paperwork. "Rioting and unlawful assembly. They probably attend every event together."

"And because they live together, they'll use each other as alibis," Charlotte said.

Renz turned to the officer. "Okay, I guess they're free to go. Thanks for all the help."

"Not a problem, Agent DeLeon. We'll take care of that immediately. All we need is a signature on the release forms."

Chapter 18

I grumbled all the way back to our office, where we would part ways for the night only to begin the process again first thing in the morning. During tomorrow's meeting, I planned to suggest that a press conference might be in order. Five murders in one night and probably within minutes of each other, whether the victims were homeless or not, was a significant event. The public needed to be informed of the danger since homeless people rarely made front-page news. Somebody had to have seen or heard something, just like Ray had. If only more people were as brave as he was and would come forward with what they knew.

I thought about Erik as I drove home. Even though he'd said he was sleeping at eight yesterday morning, that didn't mean it was true. I was sure he would have denied being on Hemmer Street, too, if we hadn't have had the pictures to prove it.

That's it. There have to be cameras near that duplex since stores are sprinkled throughout the area on Greenfield. If Erik was asleep at eight in the morning, there wouldn't be a chance in hell of seeing him exit the duplex or even catching an upstairs light on. Seeing him on camera walking down the street, leaving in a car, or even waiting in a bus shelter would prove he's lying. Kyle said we had to find irrefutable evidence before we could move on with him or Lucas as suspects.

I finally had something to hope for, and I looked forward to tomorrow. We would head to West Allis after our morning updates, ask around, and do our best to locate an outdoor camera that could put Erik Smalley awake and upright during the time Brandon Dalton was murdered.

It was closing in on eight o'clock by the time I arrived home. Another twelve-hour day and another weekend shot to hell. I prayed for a lottery win that would afford me a cabin on a lake with twenty acres in northern Wisconsin. I'd be as happy as possible unless the image in my mind could include my dad being there. I let out a wistful sigh, parked in the garage, and lowered the overhead door.

A bowl of soup or leftovers from Amber and Kate's dinner would be fine with me. All I wanted to do was go to bed, drift off, and hope my dreams wouldn't involve criminals.

Luckily, a pot of chili was still on a low simmer on the stove. That, a few pieces of thick garlic toast, and a beer would be my supper, and I couldn't think of anything better. The three of us had some small talk while I ate, with Spaz cozied up on Kate's lap, the perfect ending to a long day. After putting my bowl in the sink, I gave all three of them a kiss on the forehead and headed down the hallway. My king-sized bed was calling my name.

Chapter 19

Before their late-night meeting began, as they sat at the back of the building, Erik updated Jacob about the surprise visit he had gotten from law enforcement that afternoon.

"Were they officers or detectives?" Jacob asked.

"There were four of them—two men and two women—and they weren't wearing uniforms. They had the cops haul Lucas and me to the police station, where they questioned us. Those assholes had pictures of me following Brandon on Hemmer Street yesterday. I knew that kid was too ambitious for his own good. He thought he was a hotshot, got careless, and returned to the scene for whatever stupid reason. Somebody had to have seen him there, or the cops wouldn't have been looking for him."

"Hmm... maybe detectives, then."

"Wait a minute. I remember the guy saying that their agents were searching the apartment."

"Agents, huh? That means the FBI is already involved. Probably because five people died within a short time of each other and in five different police jurisdictions. They obviously know the murders are connected, but now we'll really get them scrambling. You did put the gun back where you got it from, right?"

"Absolutely. The FBI thought they were going to scare me with their search warrant tactics, but the duplex doesn't have anything inside that'll help them. It's a typical guys' apartment filled with dirty clothes, dirty dishes, and empty beer bottles."

"You did good, Erik. Now let's see how proud you'll make me tonight. Are you ready to head out?"

"You bet I am. That lady won't know what hit her."

"Remember to always keep the gloves on no matter what. I'll pass out the weapons you'll use in a minute." Jacob turned his wrist. "Let's go back inside. I need to call our meeting to order." After returning to the makeshift stage made of pallets, Jacob and Evelyn sat down. "Is everyone in attendance?" Jacob counted heads by jabbing the air in front of each attendee.

Micah, in the second row, looked around. "I don't see Brandon."

"Brandon bowed out," Evelyn said. "He had a change of heart. Now, shall we get started?"

Jacob went over the instructions in great length for each of the four remaining recruits and Erik, as was discussed in secret that morning between Brandon, Evelyn, and himself. Erik would take over Brandon's duties.

The basket was passed around, and each recruit pulled out a homemade garrote.

"Do all of you know how to use the garrotes?" Evelyn asked.

They nodded.

"Okay, then. Each one of you has a target that you've studied up on. You know their name, their face, and why they were chosen. The location where you'll find them is in your notes. We deliberately picked people who are out and about in the late evening so nobody has to risk their own safety by breaking into homes." Evelyn slapped her hands together. "Any questions before we send you out into the world?"

"Who's taking Brandon's place?" Micah asked.

Erik spoke up. "I volunteered since I was his handler."

"But I thought nobody was allowed to bow out after that first night."

Jacob took over. "Brandon was the only exception, and he swore he'd never talk about us or our plans to anyone. I have complete confidence that he'll never utter a word. The rest of you have come too far, so bowing out isn't an option anymore. Everyone stay invisible, be careful, and we'll gather at the South Barclay Street location tomorrow night at ten o'clock. We're getting close, and you'll learn the identity of the real targets then." Jacob gave Erik a nod, then everyone left the building.

Chapter 20

Erik had his assignment memorized and knew exactly where to park to stay out of sight of his target and the restaurant cameras. He would watch from the parallel parking spot he'd chosen a half block away. The woman had to walk to the employees' parking lot, which was right around the corner from the restaurant. It was also in perfect view of where Erik had parked.

He arrived fifteen minutes before she would leave. He knew her schedule. The restaurant stopped serving at nine and closed at ten, and she stuck around until the last employee went home. She'd kill the lights, set the alarm, and lock the door just after eleven. With her leaving last and her car being the only one in the lot, there would be no mistaking his target for anyone else.

Erik could easily hide behind the trash bins, approach her from the back, and wrap the garrote around her neck, but the singular pole lamp positioned in the middle of the lot would give away the attack. He was well-aware of that risk and not willing to take it. He would hit her car as she drove toward the lake. There were plenty of side roads that snaked around the homes in that remote area northeast of the city along Lake Michigan's shores. Earlier, he'd decided on Hidden Cove Way just because it was on her way home and he liked the name. He'd ram her car down the deep ravine and kill her once she was physically stunned.

The anticipation almost made him giddy, especially since he'd been able to stop the FBI in their tracks that morning. They had nothing on him. Their team didn't find one shred of incriminating evidence in his apartment, and he, as well as those amateur agents, knew it.

Erik stared blankly out the windshield until movement caught his eye. It was her, and she was headed to the parking lot. He whispered in enthusiasm. "Here we go. It's showtime." Erik watched as she unlocked the door of her midsized sedan and climbed in. Seconds later, she exited the parking lot and turned right, and when she was halfway down the block, he pulled out. According to his online search, she lived six and a half miles north of the restaurant in a cottage overlooking the lake. The area was densely wooded, and ravines were plentiful. The narrow roads leading to the cottages weaved around those deep dips. He would go with his plan to run her off the road then come to her rescue as if he'd seen a hit-and-run vehicle speed away. Then he'd pull out the garrote, wrap it around her neck, and twist the handles. Erik would drag her to his car, toss her body in the trunk, and drive to a sketchy area of Milwaukee, where sooner or later, she would be found by drug dealers, thieves, or somebody with a less than desirable reputation.

He looked in his rearview mirror at the city fading fast behind him. The woman's taillights were a half dozen car lengths ahead with no cars between them. After she made several turns onto those back country roads, he would strike. Nobody would be around to witness his actions, and as long as he got to her before she could call for help, she'd be at his mercy.

Twenty minutes later, he saw her pump the brakes several times before the right turn signal blinked.

We're getting close. Only a few miles to go. Two more turns and then I'll smash into the back of her car and send her careening into a ravine.

Erik pressed the gas pedal deeper to the floor and sped up. She turned right and then left, and he saw his opportunity. An S curve was coming up with deep ravines on both sides of the road. He gunned it, jerked the steering wheel to the right, and smacked the driver's rear quarter panel. He slammed on the brakes so he wouldn't get tangled in her spinning car. Her tires hit the shoulder, causing gravel to spray everywhere. The small stones pelted his windshield like summer hail.

Erik involuntarily flinched. "Damn it!" He caught sight of her car just as it teetered on the edge of the shoulder then slid on its side into the ravine.

"Perfect! Now to help her out of the vehicle like the concerned citizen I am."

Erik jammed the garrote into his pocket, put on the gloves, and inched down the hill while yelling out to the woman.

"Hello, hello! I'm coming down the hill to help you. I just called 911, and they're on their way." Erik reached the passenger-side door and yanked it open.

The dazed, bloodied woman turned her head as she fumbled with her words. "What happened? Who are you? Did you cause this?"

"No, ma'am, but I saw the vehicle that ran you off the road. Let me get you out before the gas fumes overtake us. Can you unfasten your seat belt?"

"Um, maybe, but I'm so disoriented."

"That's because your car is lying on its side. Your door won't open, so you'll have to crawl over the console to reach me. I'll help you up the hill."

Her agonized moans nearly made Erik laugh.

You haven't seen anything yet.

"Grab my hands. We have to hurry."

"Thank you. I don't know what I'd do without your help. Nobody would have seen my car down here."

Erik silently snickered.

That was the plan, idiot.

He took her hands and, with a pull, got her out of the car and to her feet.

She wobbled then looked back. "Wait, my purse and phone."

"Let's get up the hill. I'll come back with my flashlight and find them for you."

"Thank you. You're truly a lifesaver."

He grinned. "I'll be right behind you, but you need to grab every root and branch you can to pull yourself up. We don't need you sliding back down the ravine."

It took nearly a half hour to get her up to the road, and as soon as he did, Erik pulled the garrote from his pocket. There wasn't a logical reason to kill her in the ravine and drag dead weight all the way up the hill. While she was exhausted, he acted with lightning speed. He looped the cord around her neck, then he twisted the handles.

Even in her confused and injured state, she did her best to fight him off. She swatted the air behind her head. Erik leaned back. He couldn't allow her fingernails to connect with his face and leave claw marks. She scratched at her neck and thrashed with every ounce of energy she had, which was minimal. It didn't take long. Erik felt the fight leave her body as she went limp. He gave the handles another twist and held the pressure for a minute longer just to make sure.

"There, that ought to do it."

He let go. Her knees buckled, and she dropped to the ground. Erik popped the trunk, opened the emergency tool kit, and pocketed the flashlight. After scanning the road, Erik dragged her to the car, lifted her over the back bumper, and dropped her into the trunk. He scurried down the hill again and, with the help of the flashlight, quickly found her phone and purse. He couldn't linger there any longer, and within ten minutes, he was behind the wheel and heading to the wrong side of the tracks with her dead body in his trunk.

Chapter 21

I woke up feeling refreshed and raring to go. I didn't feel the need to ride the snooze button since I'd had nine hours of uninterrupted sleep and not a single bad guy had entered my dreams. The day was starting out just right. I was out of the house fifteen minutes early because it was Monday, the first workday of most people's week, and for some unknown reason, the day many of those people forgot how to drive. I was sure that data had been collected about which workday had the most car accidents, and in my few months of driving to St. Francis, I'd found that Mondays were typically the day I walked in late. I vowed to do better and promised Maureen I would. I crossed my fingers and hoped nobody would be texting while driving the freeway to work that morning.

Fifty minutes later, I wore a wide grin as I crossed our parking lot. I got to work in record time, which gave me an extra minute to grab a coffee on my way to the office I shared with Renz. I was sure our newest case would start moving along if we could spot Erik outside yesterday morning, either near his house or in the area where Brandon was found. Even if they went to that alley together, Erik had to find a way home. We would check every exit around the Miller Street alley and look for cameras on apartment buildings, doorbells, or storefronts. Somebody shot Brandon and either walked away or was picked up by an accomplice, but without camera evidence, we were dead in the water.

In the lunchroom, I fed the coffee machine three quarters and waited as the brew poured into a Styrofoam cup. Somebody would start a pot sooner or later, but I wanted to sip hot coffee as I put together my thoughts for our morning meeting. I walked to our office and, after opening the door, was surprised to see that Renz wasn't there. I checked the time—7:47, still thirteen minutes before our eight o'clock meeting.

Where the hell did he go? He wasn't in the lunchroom.

I stuck my head out the door and looked from left to right—nobody anywhere.

Hmm... maybe they started the meeting early, but why would they?

With my coffee in hand, I grabbed a notepad and pen and headed to the conference room. I was surprised to see four of my colleagues and Taft gathered around the table and deep in a speakerphone call. Renz looked up, put his finger to his mouth, then pulled out a chair for me. I sat down, remained quiet, and listened to the back-and-forth conversation. Even though I'd come in midway through the call, I picked up on the urgency. Taft was talking to the chief of police from the District 1 State Street station. What I'd walked in on sounded like a desperate plea for help.

According to him and the four other police chiefs that he had spoken with during the late-night hours, five more people had been murdered overnight. I couldn't believe what I was hearing—five more dead bodies. That number had to be relevant to the killers, yet because Milwaukee County had seven police precincts, I wondered if the killers had hit the same ones as before, or were they rotating districts? I was sure to learn more after the call ended, but from what I could piece together, it sounded like the murder victims that time were everyday people, not homeless tent dwellers.

My mind was going a million miles an hour. Were the killers advancing their agenda? Did they even have an agenda, or were they killing purely for the sake of killing? Had they become more daring since it was glaringly obvious that we had no idea who'd killed the five homeless people? Or was I wrong on all fronts and the murders were part of a well-organized plan that would shock all of Milwaukee County? I had no idea, and we had no suspects in custody and not a single motive to work with.

The conference call ended ten minutes later, but during that time, I had jotted down questions as fast as my mind could come up with them.

Maureen let out what sounded like a discouraged sigh. "Okay, only half of the team heard the entire phone call with Chief Barrett." She checked the time. "Our regular meeting will be starting in a few, so everyone grab a coffee, a notepad, do whatever you need to do, and be back in ten minutes. By then, everyone should be here. There's no reason to repeat these latest findings more than once."

We rose from the table, and Fay headed to the back counter and started a pot of coffee. I walked with Renz down the hallway toward the cafeteria, where I was sure he'd grab a morning sweet roll like he did every day.

"I'll meet you back here in five. I have to use the ladies' room."

He nodded and kept going.

Minutes later, we met in the hallway.

"Renz, what the hell is going on?"

He blew out a loud puff. "Nothing good, that's for damn sure. We've got our work cut out for us, Jade, and it has to be a group effort between all the law enforcement agencies. You didn't hear that part of the phone call, but one of the people killed last night was the mayor's daughter."

"Holy shit! Practice on the homeless and then go after the real targets? What's the mayor's daughter's story?"

He shrugged. "I don't recognize her name, so she couldn't have been a high-profile person in the city and definitely not a politician."

"So, we don't even have a 'type' of individual they're going after?"

"Don't know. The chief is sending over the police reports from every district that was hit last night, the times, the people killed, and the method of murder. We may end up in the conference room all day trying to put together a profile of the killers and their motive."

"Yeah, good luck with that. I guess what I hoped we'd be doing today is getting shoved to the back burner."

Renz nodded as we returned to our seats in the conference room. "Tell me about it later."

By that time, all eight field agents, along with Taft, were in attendance.

"Okay, everyone, I need your undivided attention," Maureen said. "I was alerted to a new development less than an hour ago, and it isn't good. It looks like five more people were brutally murdered overnight. Dave and his assistants are already going from crime scene to crime scene, trying to keep up with the carnage. In less than forty-eight hours, ten people have been murdered by unknown assailants. No group has claimed responsibility, and no witnesses have come forward. This investigation will be an all-hands-on-deck joint effort between every law enforcement agency in the county. The local police for each jurisdiction and their homicide detectives are out in force. They're interviewing everyone they can find, looking for camera footage, combing the areas for clues, and so on. We need to put together a profile of the perps and figure out their motive if we're ever going to get ahead of the killing. There's no indication they'll continue with the massacre, but there's also no indication that they'll stop. And since serial crimes is our unit, whether we're in a different state or right here in our own community, it's our expertise, and we need to get ahead of this before the county ends up on lockdown and panic sets in."

Maureen asked if we had any questions, and I knew that since we wouldn't have the opportunity to act on my idea, I presented it to our group in hopes that she might suggest the local police take action on it.

"Ma'am?"

"Yes, Jade, go ahead."

"This idea was something I was going to suggest for today, but in light of these new developments, I agree that our expertise is better used for figuring out who is committing the murders. I believe the local police districts can handle my idea."

"Sure, go ahead."

"I was going to suggest that since Erik Smalley is the only person of interest so far, we dig deeper into his alibi of being asleep yesterday during the time frame when Brandon Dalton was shot. Whoever killed Brandon exited that alley by either cutting through yards or having a ride out. I think checking footage from every camera the police can find in the area, as well as around Erik's apartment, may prove useful. If Erik is seen leaving that duplex yesterday morning any time prior to eight a.m., well, that ruins his alibi of being asleep during that time."

"I agree, and I'll contact the police chiefs from both of those districts and get them started on that. Great idea, Jade."

"Thank you, ma'am." I took a sip of coffee, cleared my throat, and continued. "I also think the number five must be relevant to the killers. There has to be a reason why five people were murdered each time. There also has to be a reason that, except in Brandon's case, all the victims were killed at night. It could be as simple as darkness giving the killer better cover, so who knows."

"And less likely for anyone to make a positive ID," Carl said.

"Good points. So, this isn't May, the fifth month, and Saturday, when the murders began, wasn't the fifth day of the month either."

Renz groaned. "Five could stand for anything like a birthday, an anniversary, or maybe five horrible things happened in the past in those districts."

Fay spoke up. "Were they the same districts both times?"

"Actually, they weren't. So that isn't a factor or at least not a major one," Taft said.

Charlotte took her turn. "What about the latest victims? Birthdates, addresses? Are they twenty-five or possibly fifty-five years old? Do they have five siblings or five kids? We can speculate forever."

Maureen held up her hand. "I know, I know. So we're pretty sure the homeless people, as sad as it sounds, were used as practice for the ones who were murdered last night. Do we all agree on that?" She looked at each of us as we nodded. "Then we need a plan of action and progress from there. First, we'll tear apart the lives of last night's victims. I want to know every detail about them down to their favorite vegetable. I don't know how Mayor Kent wants to handle the news about his daughter, but I'm going to give him a call, offer my condolences, and see where he wants us to go with announcing her death to the public. He may be able to give us insight about her and her lifestyle." Maureen pushed back her chair and stood. "I'll be back soon. Meanwhile, learn everything you can about those victims."

Chapter 22

We rose from the table, went to our offices, and returned with our laptops. We had five victims to investigate, and I hoped we'd find the link that made them targets. That would involve learning more about their friends, family, jobs, political viewpoints, living arrangements, and their lifestyles. Since we didn't know what caused them to become the chosen targets, it was imperative that we dig into every aspect of their lives.

We passed around the initial police reports to see if we could find similarities in where they were killed, the time they were killed, and the manner of death.

After comparing all of them to each other, Renz tapped the last report with his pen. "The reports say there were cuts, scrapes, and lacerations to the neck of every victim. What they don't say is that their throats were slashed."

"Sounds like strangulation, then." I thought about the necktie killer who'd terrorized southeast Wisconsin several years ago, but the description of lacerations and cuts didn't match that MO. Someone being strangled would typically fight back and possibly cut their own neck as they clawed at the tool used to strangle them. "And just like in the homeless murders, no weapons were found."

We gathered the information from the internet, then Tommy read the victims' profiles. Tamara Kent was the mayor's unmarried thirty-one-year-old daughter, who was employed at Dalia's, an upscale restaurant where she was the night shift manager. There was Pete Lawrence, a forty-seven-year-old mechanic who had a wife and two teenage daughters. Sheila Kam was a sixty-year-old cashier who worked nights at a big-box grocery store. Amanda Kennedy, a nineteen-year-old, lived with her parents and worked as a server at Silver Shores Resort on Kensington Boulevard. Finally, there was George Patrick, a night shift foreman at a kitchen appliance factory. He was single and thirty-eight.

Mike shook his head. "I don't get it. There isn't one victim who seems to have a connection to anyone else. None of the age groups match, and neither do their occupations."

"There is one common denominator—they all worked at night," Fay said.

Kyle agreed. "Making them easy prey, but the killers would have to know that information ahead of time. Again, not random killings."

Taft returned to the conference room several minutes later and took her seat at the head of the table. "Guess the word is already out that the mayor's daughter is dead. Mayor Kent is going to make a public statement later this afternoon. He doesn't know how she was murdered, only that she was. The police have already spoken with her coworkers. We're waiting for Dave's evaluation of the COD for all of last night's victims, which, again, will not be released to the public, especially if the method is the same for every death." Maureen looked at me. "I spoke with the police chiefs from District Two, which covers Erik's home, and District Six, where the alley is that Brandon was discovered in. They're going to assign officers around the clock to check into sightings of Erik both outside and in the area of his home before eight a.m. They'll also look for anyone coming out of that alley between seven and eight o'clock yesterday morning and let us know what they find."

Renz took his turn. "So far, just from the brief internet searches we've conducted, all five people were night shift workers, but other than that, there was really nothing that we'd consider factors they had in common."

Maureen wrote that down. "Check into extracurricular activities such as art classes, musical instruments they might have played, gym memberships, sporting activities, and political or addiction groups. Run the whole gamut."

I frowned, and Maureen noticed. She pointed at me. "Go ahead with whatever you're thinking."

"The reason has to be personal, something deep and painful to the killers."

"So you think these are vigilante killings—a personal vendetta?"

"I think so. Who would be mad at people who shared a common love of music or the arts?"

"Hmm. I see your point."

"Can't be, Jade," Carl said.

"Why not?"

"Because who would have a vendetta against all five people who have nothing in common? How could the five of them, who likely didn't know one another—"

I interrupted. "We don't know that yet."

"Okay, I stand corrected. How could someone have a grudge against all of those victims who *probably* didn't know each other and came from different walks of life? They'd had to have conspired to do something as a group against the killer or killers for them to feel retaliation was in order."

"All right. We're getting way ahead of ourselves. What's most important is finding out what connects these people to each other and to the killers. We need to learn who each victim's acquaintances were, talk to everyone they knew as friends, foes, workmates, or family, and then start putting the puzzle pieces together. We'll go out as far as first cousins on the family side of it, but for now, we'll start with their inner circles and work our way out." Maureen's phone rang, and we all went quiet while she talked. "Yes, Dave, what's the verdict?" We watched as she rubbed her brow and shook her head. "And there's no mistaking the marks? Okay, and TOD?" She jotted down numbers, thanked him, and hung up. "Wow. Just wow."

We remained silent while she seemed to be gathering her thoughts.

Taft let out a long breath, sat up straight, and addressed us. "Dave's best guess is that all five of last night's victims were killed with some type of garrote."

I pulled back. "What the—"

She held up her hands, and Renz elbowed me.

I immediately apologized. "Sorry, Maureen, that's just shocking to hear. Can you actually purchase them, or are they all homemade?"

Maureen shrugged. "I'm not sure on that yet, Jade, but we'll dig into it. Continuing on, Dave puts the time of death for all the victims between ten p.m. and midnight. What we'll have to check out is when each one of them ended their work shift and if they went anywhere else before going home since we know their murders didn't take place at their residences. The police departments are looking for camera footage at each workplace to see if a vehicle followed the victim after they left work."

"As if the perp was lying in wait," Fay said.

"And I'm sure they were. Because most workplaces have cameras, they probably didn't want to take the chance of the attack being recorded."

Renz scratched his cheek then added his opinion. "So the victims' vehicles weren't at the site where they were found?"

"The police haven't located the vehicles yet. I'm assuming when they do, they'll see that they were somehow disabled or the perp hit the car deliberately and then attacked the occupant." Maureen sighed. "For now, divide up the victims' contacts however you want, go interview them in depth about every aspect of their loved one's life, and then we'll compare the information later. Meanwhile, there are BOLOs out for the missing vehicles. Once they're located, that in itself should tell us something."

Chapter 23

Once we had the names and addresses for each victim's immediate family, we headed out. Renz and I took Tamara Kent's case. Since the mayor was a high-profile politician in Milwaukee, we needed to address his daughter's murder immediately. We'd found out that he had left his office and returned home, but I wasn't sure who we should speak with first—him or Tamara's friends and coworkers.

Since the police had already called on and interviewed the people who had worked during Tamara's shift last night, Renz suggested we head to the mayor's home instead. We would follow up with everyone else later.

The Kent's were expecting us, thanks to Taft's earlier conversation with the mayor where she'd mentioned that FBI agents would be calling. Renz turned onto the driveway and pulled up to the intercom next to the gate. He pressed the call button and waited. We weren't sure who answered, only that the woman said it was the Kent residence. After Renz explained who we were, she told him to park next to the portico and released the gate. He pulled ahead.

Mayor Kent and his wife, Marie, lived on the swanky

east side. Their estate, like the others in that neighborhood, had sweeping views of Lake Michigan. In front of us stood a traditional redbrick colonial home with stately white pillars and beautifully manicured gardens. The mansion appeared to be one of the originals on that block by the looks of the neighboring homes that were also gated and just as stately.

"Wow. How much is the mayor's annual salary?" I asked, stunned by the opulence.

Renz shrugged. "Couple hundred thousand a year, I'd imagine."

I huffed. "You aren't going to own this compound on that income."

"I'm pretty sure Mayor Kent comes from old money. If I remember correctly, his grandfather started one of the local breweries well over a hundred years ago."

"Humph." I pointed at the portico. "Guess that's where you're supposed to park."

"Yep, I see it." Renz parked, and we got out. I grabbed my briefcase from the back seat, then we headed up the brick sidewalk.

I clacked the brass lion's-head door knocker against the thick wooden door, and we waited. A woman who appeared to be in her late fifties pulled open the door. I assumed from her swollen red eyes that I was staring at the face of Marie Kent.

"Mrs. Kent?"

"Yes, that's me, and apparently you're the FBI agents."

"That's correct, ma'am. I'm SSA Jade Monroe, and this

is my partner, SSA Lorenzo DeLeon."

Marie backed away from the door to allow us through. "Please come in, Agents. Michael is in the library." She pointed to her left. "Right this way."

We followed Mrs. Kent into a well-appointed library, where her husband, the mayor, sat at his desk with the chair facing the window. He stared out over the expansive lake. As I knew well, the water was hypnotizing with its tankers, barges, and sailboats passing by. On a windy day, seagulls rode the whitecapped waves.

"Michael, the FBI agents are here to speak with us."

He rose from the chair. I noticed a bottle of bourbon on the desk and an empty glass sitting next to it. I hoped he hadn't already begun drinking that morning—it was only ten o'clock. We needed him sober and coherent, but we did have Marie, too, and although she was a mess, she seemed completely sober.

The mayor rounded the desk and shook our hands as Renz made the introductions.

He tipped his head toward the door. "Let's sit in the living room where it's more comfortable, shall we?"

We walked with them to the living room, two rooms away. That room also faced the lake, but luckily, the sheer curtains were still drawn. I was glad there wouldn't be outside distractions as we asked our questions.

We sat across from the couple, on a matching leather sofa, and began by offering our condolences. The mayor nodded his appreciation.

"Do you have any information yet, Agents, and please

call me Mike. I prefer to be informal in my own home."

Renz took the lead. "Mike, I don't know if you were notified of the brutal murders of homeless people that happened around the two a.m. hour Saturday morning."

He stared at us with a bewildered expression. "No, I don't know anything about that, but what does it have to do with Tamara? She was our only child, for God's sake. We need to find her killer and bring him to justice."

"It's a bit more complicated than that, sir."

"How? Don't police detectives and FBI agents find murderers all the time?"

I spoke up. "There are many murderers roaming the streets who have never been apprehended, Mayor Kent."

He swatted the air. "Was that comment supposed to make me feel confident in law enforcement's ability?"

Marie frowned. "Michael, please, they're trying to help."

I instantly regretted making that comment.

Renz took over. "Sir, those five innocent people were murdered during the early hours of Saturday, and then five more people were killed last night, including your daughter."

"My God, what are you saying?" Marie asked.

"We're saying that Tamara wasn't the only person murdered, and once again, it was five people who lost their lives."

"How did they die? Were they together? Did they all die at once, in the same manner? Tell us what's going on."

"Sir, we believe the ten people killed in the last forty-eight hours were at the hands of at least two individuals, maybe more. They have an agenda, a wrong to right, and this is the time they decided to act on that vendetta, if you will."

"A vendetta against our daughter? She was a restaurant manager. Did somebody dislike the food at Dalia's?"

"No, ma'am. We don't believe any of the victims were acquainted with each other, and we don't believe the murders had anything to do with their occupations. The only people who knew why they were chosen were the killers."

"What about witnesses?"

"Because none of the cars have been found and all the bodies were located in less than desirable neighborhoods, we believe the killers are doing their best to make our investigation as difficult as possible. There are four other families who are grieving, too, and we need to find out if the victims had connections with each other that none of us are aware of. That's why we're here. We need to know everything about Tamara's life that you can think of."

Marie frowned. "You mean her daily activities, where she went, who she talked to?"

"We realize you wouldn't know all of that, but anything you can give us will help put the puzzle pieces together."

"Okay, well, Tamara called me every morning around ten a.m. as she cooled down from her morning run."

"And she ran alone?"

"She did as far as I know." Marie rubbed her forehead. "I always worried about that since she lives in a rural area north of here along the lake. Mostly weekend cottages tucked back in the woods. Did someone—"

"Ma'am, we don't know where Tamara was killed since we have no idea where her car is at. We have BOLOs out for every victim's vehicle. There could be evidence of a deliberate hit to the car, which is a ruse criminals often use to either abduct people, rob them, or carjack the vehicle."

Marie pulled a tissue from the dispenser on the coffee table and dabbed her eyes.

"What else besides the daily phone call after her run? Did she go to a gym too?"

Mike said she didn't. "She does take business classes at UWM twice a week, though. Eventually, she wants to open her own restaurant."

Marie covered his hand with her own. "She *wanted* to open a restaurant, but now that will never happen." Her voice caught in her throat, and she sobbed openly.

"Did Tamara have a steady boyfriend or someone who might have been more than just a friend? Also, was there anyone she spoke of who was angry with her—an employee or a neighbor, maybe?"

Marie shook her head. "Nobody that she spoke of to us."

I glanced down at my notes. "Okay, so she ran every morning, and she took business classes at UWM. Anything else?"

"Other than having a normal social life, no. She went out with her friends on occasion, whether they were work friends or people she knew from her classes. She traveled, she obviously loved to cook and entertained now and then, but that's all I can think of," Marie said.

"How often did you see her?" Renz asked.

Marie shook her head. "I probably saw her more than Michael did since I don't work outside the home. I guess I saw her twice a week. Sometimes, she'd come over for supper on the weekends if she wasn't working since that's about the only time she'd see her dad."

I nodded as I wrote. "Do you have a key to her cottage?"

"We do."

"May we borrow it? We'd like to take a look inside to see if there are any clues before you start going through it."

"I suppose so."

"Also, do you know her running route?"

Marie nodded. "Yes, it was a two-mile loop around the street she lived on from her house on Lake Vista to Oak Ridge Drive and then a right on Hidden Cove Way. That circles back to Lake Vista Road."

"Okay, thank you. I guess that's everything we need for now except the key. We'll make sure to get it back to you in the next few days. Again, we're so sorry for your loss," Renz said.

"Agents?"

Renz looked back. "Yes, Mike?"

"When can we see her?"

Renz rubbed his chin. "Give us a few days. I promise we'll reach out when the time is right."

Chapter 24

Evelyn poured a second cup of coffee for both of them and returned to the table. She let out a sigh as she took her seat and stared at the chart Jacob had created.

"Do you think they're suffering yet?"

"Of course they are. We did, and you do remember how that felt, right?"

She nodded. "I can't believe five months and five days have passed already." She covered Jacob's hand with her own. "I also can't believe we've been strong enough to survive it. I do feel bad about the homeless people, though—"

Jacob shushed her. "It was necessary, Evie. Do you really think they were living their best lives? Most homeless people are mentally challenged, drug abusers, or alcoholics. Their families have thrown them out and abandoned them. Why do you think they end up homeless and have nothing but their own wits to get by on? I'm sure some commit suicide too." Jacob sighed. "Anyway, we needed to make sure we had reliable, trustworthy people who would get the job done. They had to prove themselves." He tapped the chart with his index finger. "We're almost there, so don't start second-guessing the plan. Those people covered everything up as if it never happened and we didn't matter. They're the criminals, and now it'll be exposed in the worst way they'd ever imagine. When it's all said and done, they'll pay their dues."

"But what about Romans 12:19?"

Jacob wagged his finger at his wife. "There are all kinds of Bible passages you can quote. What about an eye for an eye? Yet there's the turn-the-other-cheek quote too. Now isn't the time to backpedal on what we're doing. It's too late to stop. It's close to the end, and God will forgive us if we're sincere in asking for it. Have faith in that."

Evelyn took a sip of coffee and stared into her cup. "Have you seen the news?"

"Yes, and they're saying only what they have to. Those FBI agents Erik spoke of are keeping a tight lid on the real facts. They don't want the manner of death to get out, and they certainly aren't going to give away their theories."

"Do you think they actually have a theory?"

"Of course they do, but they're so far off they'll never figure it out. We'll complete our mission without anyone ever putting the puzzle pieces together. The people responsible may never be exposed for the corrupt trash they are, unless the truth gets out, but we'll still have the satisfaction of ridding them from this world."

"I can't wait until that day of reckoning. Maybe after five months of anguish, I'll be able to sleep through the night again," Evelyn said.

"I hope so, honey."

Chapter 25

We reached the cottage on Lake Vista Road and pulled into the short gravel driveway. I immediately noticed that there wasn't a garage, so there would be no reason to wonder whether Tamara's car was there or not. The cute cottage had white clapboard siding and dark-green shutters. A ground-to-rooftop stone fireplace accented the left side of the home, and wooden shake shingles topped the roof. The small yard was full of flower beds, some still with color, and the grass was a vibrant green. I imagined that in several months, everything would be covered in a blanket of snow, including the huge pine trees that lined the road in front of the home. The place was a gem and something I would long for as a weekend retreat.

"Well?"

I nodded as I opened the passenger-side door. "Yep, no time like the present."

We walked the slate sidewalk to the front door only thirty feet from the car. Renz turned the key in the dead bolt and pushed open the door.

The home was as neat as a pin. Business course books

lay on the coffee table, a bowl of fresh fruit was centered on the breakfast bar, and the refrigerator was fully stocked. The cottage was only a one-bedroom, one-bath home, but it was decorated thoughtfully and looked cozy and inviting.

My mind went to the image of Tamara lying on a filthy mattress in an abandoned house in one of the worst neighborhoods of Milwaukee. We hadn't been to the actual scene, but we did see photographs from all five murders, and none of the victims deserved the fate that was so violently chosen for them. I shook my head to clear my mind. I needed to look for clues, but since four other people had been killed in the same manner, I knew the likelihood of finding any incriminating evidence was extremely low. I entered the bedroom, and the bed had been made. There weren't even clothes strewn across the upholstered wingback chair that sat under the window facing the rear of the house.

"Wow, she was truly a neatnik, but I guess that isn't so hard to do when you live alone." I glanced at Renz. "Right?"

He shrugged. "I'm pleading the fifth."

I grinned. "I think our time is better served walking the route she ran every day."

"Why? We know she went to work last night and clocked out shortly after eleven once all the employees had left. It's not like she was going to go for a run late at night, and her car would have been here if that was the case."

I grumbled as I gave the house another quick scan. "You're right, and it isn't like there's signs of a break-in. Let's lock up and just drive the route before we leave."

Renz rolled his eyes. "Whatever. Let's take a look out back and in the mailbox first."

We rounded the cottage to a wide view of Lake Michigan. The wind on that side of the house was brisk, and far below the bluff where we stood, whitecaps dotted the water's surface.

"How beautiful is this?"

Renz shielded his eyes and looked out over the lake. "Pretty beautiful."

I sighed. "Okay, back to the real world of gritty locations and dead bodies."

After looking in the empty mailbox we climbed into the cruiser and headed down Lake Vista Road until it intersected with Oak Ridge Drive. We drove it for a half mile and saw Hidden Cove Way. I pointed at the road sign. "Make a right turn there, Renz. Isn't that a pretty name for a road?"

"It is, and everything out here is pretty too. I bet even a small cottage like Tamara's goes for three hundred thousand or more."

I had to agree. "Probably more."

Renz weaved around the two-lane roads. The entire area was wooded with a mix of oak, maple, and pine trees. The sugar maples were the first to change colors, and the vibrant reds, yellows, and oranges were beautiful. As I stared into the woods, I understood why Tamara ran that route—it was peaceful and quiet. I would have loved to walk the two-mile distance and take in nature, but we were on the clock and had other people to interview.

Renz rounded the final curve where Hidden Cove Way met Lake Vista Road. When a flash of sunlight bounced off something through the trees, I looked across to the other side of the deep ravine. I jerked my head over my right shoulder.

"What's wrong?"

"I saw something, or should I say the sunlight bounced off something. Back up, Renz."

He shifted into Reverse and backed up slowly. "Tell me when to stop."

I held up my hand until I saw that ray of light again. "Stop now and kill the engine. We need to check out whatever that is." As soon as the car was stopped, I leapt out and looked over the shoulder's edge. "A car is down there!"

He rounded the nose of our car and stood at my side. "Damn it. What color was Tamara's car?"

"Um… I don't remember. All my notes are in my briefcase."

Renz dialed the Kent home while I looked for the best way to descend the steep hillside. He hung up seconds later.

"Well?"

"Marie said Tamara's car was cranberry red."

"And so is that one. Let's go."

"How?"

"Sit on your ass and scoot down. There are plenty of roots and limbs to hang on to."

Renz reached in his pockets and pulled out the contents.

"What are you doing?"

"Putting everything that's important back in the car in

case something falls out of my pockets."

I patted my own pockets. "I'm good."

He was back in seconds. "Okay, just sit on our asses and scoot, huh?"

"It's probably the safest way. Lower center of gravity than standing."

It took a good fifteen minutes to get to the bottom of the wooded ravine, but we reached the car unscathed. The vehicle was lying on the driver's side and butted against a large maple tree. I wondered if the passenger-side door had been opened since it was unlatched. Nobody and nothing of value was inside except the keys, which were still in the ignition, and what looked like blood on the steering wheel. I popped the glove box in hopes of finding an insurance card and did.

"Look at this. It's definitely Tamara's car, and she was less than a mile from home." I pushed through the thick brush to look all the way around the car, but because it was lying on its side, there wasn't anything we could see on the driver's side.

Renz scratched his head. "That really sucks."

"Which part in particular?"

"The part that may have shown us how the car ended up down here. If she was run off the road by the perp, then likely there would have been damage to the left rear quarter panel, but now there's no way to know if the damage to that side was from a hit or from careening down the hillside. We need to get a truck with a tow cable out here." Renz reached in his pocket. "Damn it. My phone is in the car."

I chuckled. "You probably wouldn't have gotten a signal in this gully anyway."

We held onto tree roots and pulled ourselves back up the hill, then I brushed as much dirt off my clothes as I could while Renz called Taft.

"She's sending out a tow truck, so we'll have to wait here until it comes."

"So the killer followed her almost all the way home. They're working awfully hard to stage the victims. I mean, if the intent is to kill them, then just do it. Why hide the vehicle and then move the body?"

Renz swatted the dirt from his pants as he answered. "Because they want the bodies found and the families to feel anguish. It's bad enough to have a family member murdered, but then to dispose of them like trash is even worse."

I nodded. "Plus, nobody would know exactly where they were killed." I jerked my chin at the ravine. "Except in this case. Once that car went down the hill, there was no way that it was coming back up."

"But the killer somehow got Tamara out of the ravine, which couldn't have been easy."

"Unless there was more than one of them." I frowned. "I wonder how many killers there actually are."

Chapter 26

The tow truck arrived at eleven fifteen. Renz directed the driver to stop behind our vehicle, then he walked to the driver's-side window.

"You call for a tow?"

"Not exactly. We need you to pull a vehicle up out of that ravine." Renz showed the driver his FBI badge. "We need the car on level ground, and then we'll take it from there. Our crime lab's flatbed is en route too."

"Sure. Why don't you show me what we've got." The driver climbed out of the truck and walked to the shoulder's edge with Renz. "Damn, that car is down there all right. I think it's doable, though. Just have to release the steel cable, go down there with it and attach it to the undercarriage. I guess it doesn't matter what kind of condition the car ends up in since it's pretty trashed already."

Renz shook his head. "The least amount of additional damage the better. We have to go over the car forensically."

"Hmm… maybe I can flip it back on its tires and pull it up. I'll give it a try."

"Thanks. That would be great."

After the cable was secured to the steering wheel, the driver was able to pull the car into its upright position. He scurried down the hill and repositioned the winch to the car's undercarriage. Once again in the truck, he dragged the car up the side of the ravine through brush, tree limbs, and over large roots.

Renz and I stared at the vehicle as it sat on the roadway. All of the window glass was broken out on the driver's side, dents covered nearly every surface, and the entire vehicle had twigs and leaves jammed into every opening.

"Good enough?" the tow truck driver asked.

"Absolutely. I'm assuming the charges were taken care of over the phone?"

"You bet. It's all good."

We thanked him, and he drove away. Renz checked the time. We still had to wait for the flatbed to arrive, and hours were slipping away when we could have been interviewing Tamara's workmates. Most of those evening employees started work at three o'clock, and noon had come and gone. I doubted that the car could tell us anything unless, by some miracle, the killer had left fingerprints behind. Even if Forensics could say with one hundred percent certainty that the vehicle was pitted from the rear driver's side, we still didn't know who followed her there and forced her over the edge.

We finally heard the lumbering sound of the flatbed heading our way. Renz tipped his wrist and checked the time.

"Doubt that we'll get any interviews in today. I'll find

out what Taft wants us to do."

Renz paced up and down the road as I spoke with the flatbed driver. I watched as he winched the car, for the third time that day, and pulled it up on the ramp to the truck's flat surface. There, he chained it down and said he was heading to the county's crime lab garage. I signed the release form, and he drove away.

I saw Renz walking my way. "So?"

"So, Taft said to head back. She's calling everyone in, we'll discuss what we've learned, try to make some sense of it, and go from there."

"Sounds like a plan." I headed to the passenger door.

"Jade?"

"Yep?"

"Good job seeing the car."

I grinned. "Thanks, partner."

We pulled through our headquarters' secured gate at two o'clock. After going through our security process to enter the building, we took the elevator to the third floor. Renz turned left at the hallway, and I turned right.

He looked back. "Where are you going?"

"To grab us some coffee. I'll be back in a flash."

He gave me a thank-you nod and continued on.

After pulling the hot cups from the vending machine, I secured sleeves around both of them and carried them to our office. "So, what's the word?"

"I told Taft that we were here, and she'll start the meeting as soon as everyone is back. She's figuring in a half hour."

"Good enough. So should we assume the perp was waiting outside Dalia's for Tamara to leave work last night?" I blew over my coffee and took a sip.

"That's how I see it. Is there any other way?"

"Well, sure. He could have been waiting on a side road near her house. Or it could have been a road rage incident."

Renz shook his head. "Nope, not with garrote marks on her and four other people's necks."

"Yeah, there is that. So he waited outside her work because he wasn't absolutely sure she'd go straight home."

"Yep, and then once they were back in the boondocks where nobody was around, he struck. I guess instead of hitting her and having to get rid of her car later, it was easier to have it go over the edge. Luckily, you saw the sun reflecting off the metal."

"That was pure luck. Guess I was just enjoying nature's beauty when I saw that, so don't ever complain if I'm rubbernecking out the window."

Renz chuckled. "I promise I won't."

By the time I'd thrown my Styrofoam cup in the wastebasket, it was time for our meeting. I grabbed the standard notetaking tools, and we headed down the hall. Fay, Kyle, Tommy, and Charlotte were already there. We were still waiting on Carl and Mike to show up. Taft walked in seconds later with Carl and Mike on her heels.

With the go-ahead from Taft, I began with what we'd learned that day. We already knew from the police report that Tamara Kent was an only child, unmarried, thirty-one, and lived alone in a cottage on the bluffs of Lake Michigan.

"We paid a visit to her parents, Mayor Michael Kent and his wife, Marie, who told us that Tamara worked hard as the night shift manager at Dalia's, went on a two-mile run every morning, and was taking business classes at UWM in hopes of opening her own restaurant one day. She had no enemies that they knew of, and unfortunately, we didn't have the chance to interview any of her workmates because of time constraints. We'd gone to Tamara's home with her parents' permission, did a walk-through, and found nothing amiss. As we left to continue on with the interviews, Renz drove the running route Tamara took every day from her house. As he made the final turn, I saw a flash from the sun bounce off something metallic or mirrored in a ravine that we'd just passed. Renz backed up, parked, and we walked to the shoulder's edge to check it out. At the bottom of the ravine was a car, and it appeared like it had just gone down. Renz made the phone call to ask the Kent's the color of Tamara's car. Marie said it was cranberry red, and so was the car in the ravine. Long story short, the car was Tamara's. Forensics has already taken it back to the crime lab's evidence garage. We're assuming the killer followed her from the restaurant last night but possibly scouted out her neighborhood first and realized he could use those ravines to his advantage."

Kyle huffed. "No need to get rid of her car. It was well-hidden, at least for the time being."

"Exactly. Unless Forensics finds the killer's palm or fingerprints on the car, it won't do much good as far as evidentiary value, but it does tell us a story."

Tommy agreed. "Yeah, that the killer likely knew where she lived, where she worked, and the time she ended her shift. The question still remains, why her?"

"Or why any of them?" Taft said. "We learn that and half the battle is over."

Renz took his turn. "Anyway, we'll try to make the other interviews tomorrow. Somehow, some way, those people are connected, at least in the killers' minds."

As we went around the table with everyone's reports, we learned that Pete Lawrence had a twin brother, Paul, who was a bartender. The mother was deceased, and the father walked out on the family when they were kids. Other than his wife and children, Pete's best friend was Paul, and they had done everything together. Kyle said they'd interviewed the wife, but Paul was still too distraught to talk. He said the wife couldn't think of anyone who would want to hurt Pete.

"I've heard that a twin really has a hard time when something happens to the other one," I said.

Taft nodded at Carl. "What did you guys learn?"

"That Sheila Kam was a divorced woman with an adult son and daughter. We spoke with the daughter, who lives on the east side. She's married to some high-profile attorney in town, so she was home when we came calling. The brother lives in New Mexico but is flying in tomorrow. Same answer most everyone else is getting—they can't think of anyone who would want to hurt their loved one."

Taft put eyes on Tommy and Fay. "Go ahead."

Tommy began. "We spoke with Amanda's parents, who own the resort she worked at as a server. Of course, they're beyond devastated. We also spoke with a few of Amanda's friends, who couldn't think of anyone who would harm let alone kill her."

"Charlotte? You and Kyle interviewed the foreman's neighbors, too, correct?"

Charlotte nodded at Taft. "Yes, ma'am. We spoke with a few of George Patrick's neighbors and workmates. He was a quiet guy but a good and fair boss. His mom and dad live in Florida, but they're flying in today. We talked with them on the phone, and they said George never spoke poorly of anyone, not even the employees who reported to him."

Taft squeezed her temples. "So we have five exemplary people who had great relationships with everyone and nobody has ever heard anyone speak badly of them? Is that where we're at?"

I cleared my throat. "It looks that way, ma'am."

Taft rattled her fingertips on the table. "This case doesn't jibe one bit. We're missing that big picture we spoke of a few days ago. Every victim so far except Tamara is an average, everyday person who isn't related to a high-profile individual like the mayor. Tamara doesn't fit in with that demographic other than the fact that she worked nights at a restaurant and not in the political field like her father. What if her murder didn't have anything to do with Tamara but was aimed at Michael Kent, to either send him a message or to break his heart?"

"Then what about the others?" I asked. "Why were they killed? Were their loved ones meant to suffer, too, and for what reason?"

"I can't explain it, Jade, but I think we should start with the mayor and work our way backward. Maybe it's really about him and everyone else is just a smokescreen."

I needed to change the subject for a minute and asked if the police had had any luck finding cameras around Erik's duplex or anywhere near the alley where Brandon was found. Taft said she hadn't heard back but would contact the police chiefs as soon as our meeting was over.

Maureen stood. "I'll follow up with the Erik business. What I want all of you to do first is see if any of the murder victims from last night had a relationship of any kind with the mayor. Then dig into chatter of who may have had a beef with the mayor over the last year. Start compiling names."

"But that could be anyone from all walks of life," Renz said. "They could be politicians, administrators from dozens of programs and committees, neighbors, extended family, you name it."

"And there's eight of you and an entire county of law enforcement personnel. I'd imagine every homicide detective could pitch in and lend a hand."

After Taft walked out, I stared at the door. "How in the hell are we going to perform a task that overwhelming and get any definitive answers? Everyone gets pissed at city officials. It's a fact. Then if we're working with all sorts of officers and detectives, it's going to end up being a shitstorm of monumental proportions."

Tommy took his turn. "That's why we aren't. We can handle this case ourselves. We'll go back to the families and friends of all five victims and really press for more information and find out if any of them or anyone they know has an affiliation with the mayor."

I grunted. "Well, Renz and I may as well help you guys out because we already know Tamara had an affiliation with the mayor—he was her dad."

"No," Carl said, "go press the mayor himself. If he's honest with you, he'll tell you if somebody previously had or currently has an issue with him."

Renz cocked his head. "I have to agree with Carl. Let's go back to"—he air quoted—"Kent Manor and have a very serious and candid discussion with the mayor and his wife. Especially if he realizes that Tamara's death might have been a warning to him, I'd think he'd want to be as open and helpful as possible."

Chapter 27

Everyone left and went back to speak with the same people as before. They had to dig deeper and ask tougher questions, and they would expand their interviews to even more family and acquaintances if necessary.

I made a courtesy call to the Kent home to say we were coming back with a different line of questioning for them. Mrs. Kent agreed but didn't sound enthused that we were returning. I understood mourning as much as the next person who was going through that pain. In a time of sadness, having people pry and prod for information was annoying but a necessary part of law enforcement's job.

I hung up and let out a sigh. "I don't think they want us back there."

Renz shrugged. "Do they want their daughter's killer apprehended or not?"

"I know, and I understand their feelings, but I also know what's necessary for us to do our job. It isn't always easy to find that balance."

"Well, we aren't going there to coddle anyone. I can sympathize with them, but we still have to ask the tough questions."

155

Twenty minutes later, Renz pulled up to the intercom for the second time that day, and Mrs. Kent buzzed us through. When she pulled open the door, I did a double take. Marie looked like she had aged ten years since that morning.

"Mrs. Kent, we're sorry to barge in again, but we have very important questions to ask the mayor."

She tipped her head toward the living room. "He's in there."

Renz and I passed by her and walked into the living room, where we found the mayor on a recliner with his chin resting on his chest. What appeared to be the same bottle of bourbon from that morning—with substantially less inside—sat on the table next to him along with a half-full glass. He was already well on his way to inebriation, and his head bobbed up and down like seagulls on waves as his wife called out to him. She got no response.

I looked from him to her. "Mrs. Kent?"

She shook her head. "He has a right to mourn any way he chooses, Agents."

"But we have very important questions to ask him."

"Then you should have asked them this morning when he'd only had one drink."

I sighed. "Ma'am, is there a possibility that someone has been threatening your husband? A politician, a city or county worker or administrator, a disgruntled employee, or someone who does or doesn't want a building to go up or a permit to pass? Has someone blackmailed him?"

Her expression changed, and the color drained from her

face. "I'm sure I don't know what you mean, and I don't know anything about what goes on behind closed doors in the mayor's office."

"Even to the point where your daughter's death might have happened because of an unanswered threat?"

She shrugged. "No, there's nothing you can say or do to make me believe Tamara died because Michael ignored a threat of violence or retaliation against his office or our family. He would have notified the police."

"You're sure?"

"Yes, I'm sure. Now, if you'll excuse me, and if you'd like to speak with Michael going forward, please give us twenty-four hours' notice. I'll show you out."

We thanked her and left. After she closed the door and we were out of earshot, I felt comfortable speaking freely. "She's hiding something."

Renz grunted. "Damn straight she is, and we're going to find out why. I need to run this by Taft. I think we should keep everything we find out close to the vest, leave the other agencies out of it for now to avoid a possible leak, and figure it out between the eight of us. You know the saying about six degrees of separation?"

"Yeah, I guess. It's like the small world syndrome."

"Exactly. We need to find out if any of last night's victims knew the mayor, knew somebody who knew the mayor, or were somehow related to or worked for the mayor. That can't be too hard to do."

"Should I call everyone so they press those particular questions?"

"Let me explain our theory to Taft first."

Ideas rolled around in my head like the steel balls in a pinball machine as Renz spoke with our boss. He had her on Speakerphone, but I was in my own world and knew he would explain the conversation to me later anyway. Was there really a chance that the other four victims had some connection to Michael Kent and they all died because of it? Was Marie hiding that information to protect her own ass as well as the mayor's?

Another theory popped into mind as Renz hung up. I needed to explain it to him before he began with Taft's suggestion.

"Okay, so Taft—"

"Hold up. I need to verbalize this before I forget."

"Yeah, go ahead, then."

I sucked in a deep breath. "This idea just occurred to me while you were talking with Maureen."

"So you weren't listening?"

I swatted away his comment. He knew damn well that I wasn't listening. "Just hear me out."

He nodded.

"So we know Marie is hiding information. The only reason would be to protect her and Michael, especially with what just happened to their daughter."

"Exactly, and I'm assuming Tamara's murder was meant as a warning to the mayor."

I held up my finger. "But what if Marie's silence isn't about protecting them physically?"

"I'm not following."

"What if it's about protecting the family integrity and Michael's mayoral position? What if it's about a scandal? Can you imagine the damage a scandal would do to the family dynasty, to their name, to his position in the city? He'd become a pariah, and so would she. They'd lose their standing in the community with their highfalutin friends."

Renz raised his brows. "Okay, so you mean like impropriety with an assistant or something of that nature? An employee might have witnessed an illicit deed and now wants to blackmail the mayor or extort favors or money?"

"Maybe. He does seem to drink a lot. Maybe he drinks in his office, came on to one of his staff members because he was half in the bag, and didn't think of the consequences of his actions."

"Or maybe people have seen him drinking on the job. He could be making bad decisions because of it."

I sighed. "But you'd think the deputy mayor or Michael's personal assistant would step in, fix whatever he might have messed up, and go about their day."

Renz groaned. "Maybe we're going overboard with these speculations."

"Okay, maybe we are, but something was serious enough for their daughter to be murdered over it, and I believe the others were killed to make a point. That would mean they're all connected to the mayor, one way or another."

"Yeah, the six-degree thing. Anyway, Taft said to let the others know to press on the questions about knowing the mayor and that you and I should go to Dalia's and try to interview a few people there. We don't have time to wait until tomorrow."

Chapter 28

We headed to the east side, where Dalia's was located. Renz found street parking, and although it was getting close to their suppertime rush, we needed to talk to at least a few of Tamara's closest employees.

We entered the restaurant, and a smiling hostess asked our names. Renz explained that we didn't have reservations but needed to speak with whoever was filling in for Tamara Kent. He discreetly showed the hostess his badge.

She looked around then pointed at a young man who had stepped behind the bar. "That's Derrick, and he has the most seniority. He was Tamara's second in command, so he would be the person to talk to."

We thanked her, approached Derrick, and asked to speak with him privately. He led the way to the manager's office and pointed at the set of guest chairs that faced the desk. "Please, Agents, have a seat and tell me what I can do to help. We've all been interviewed by the police already."

"We're aware of that and don't intend to ask the same questions. We know you're doing your best, and I promise we won't take up too much of your time."

"Appreciate it."

"Did Tamara ever mention feeling like she was in danger, not because of anything she had done but due to her father's position in the city?"

"Because he's the mayor?"

"Yes, exactly."

We waited as Derrick thought. After twenty seconds or so, he answered. "I don't think she ever worried about being in personal danger, but she had mentioned on several occasions that her mom seemed stressed."

"Did she say why?" I asked.

Derrick scratched his cheek. "No, but it had something to do with her dad. I don't know if she meant in a personal way or in a work capacity, though."

"Okay, anything else?"

"Not really. If her dad was in trouble, there's no way Tamara would have told anyone why. It could have leaked out. She seemed protective of her family's privacy, maybe because they're a big name in the city."

I looked at Renz. "Anything else you want to ask?"

He nodded. "Was anyone bothering Tamara here at work?"

"Not that I've ever noticed." He looked down and shook his head. "I don't know the details, only that she met with foul play, but it's a real shame. Tamara was a stand-up lady through and through. From what I've heard, her folks are taking her death really hard."

I gave Derrick one of my cards, then we thanked him and left. There was no reason to ask the employees the same questions the police had, and we were pretty sure Tamara's murder had nothing to do with her.

"Want to head back and start digging into the mayor's background?" Renz asked.

"Yep. I'm all for finding out whatever it is they're keeping secret."

Chapter 29

A smile spread across Evelyn's face when the news anchor said that the mayor had canceled the press conference he had scheduled about his daughter. He would be taking time off to mourn, needed his privacy, and couldn't address the public at that time.

"Jacob, it's working."

Evelyn's husband took a seat next to her and caught the tail end of the segment. "Good. We want everyone to go through the same gut-wrenching sadness we did."

"And they need to pay that horrific price because they participated in the cover-up. Let's take a drive."

"To where?"

"Silver Shores. I want to hear if people are talking about Amanda's murder, and we need to know if her parents are suffering like we did."

"But maybe they've temporarily closed the restaurant because of her death," Jacob said.

"And that would be even better. Then we'd truly know they're suffering. I'll call and see if they're open." Evelyn looked up the number on her phone then pressed the call button. A prerecorded message came on saying that the restaurant was closed until the following weekend due to a family tragedy. Evelyn hung up and nodded. "Good. They're in agony just like we were."

Jacob walked to the desk where the laptop sat. "I'll pull up the other names online and see if we can find any news. There has to be something for us to read that the media put together about the murders."

"How long are we going to let them wallow in their misery?"

"Before we exact our own revenge on them?"

"Yes."

"Poetic justice would be for each of them to die on the night before their loved one's funeral. That, my lovely wife, would be the shocker of the year."

Chapter 30

We had our work cut out for us. Michael Kent had been the mayor of Milwaukee since 2008 and was dug in deep. He had a lot of personal and political clout, and the chances of us learning the good, the bad, and the ugly parts of his life were great. Because any city issues that arose during his years in office were public information, news archives would have a record of them, and the media would have been sure to create a buzz. Private matters would be more difficult to uncover. Personal dirt about public officials was usually swept under the proverbial rug.

As we were about to pass Taft's office, Renz and I stopped in to give her a quick update. We told Maureen that we'd spoken with Derrick Hunt, who had been the second in charge on the evening shift at Dalia's but was taking Tamara's place.

I repeated what Derrick had said. "He told us that Tamara was worried, not for her own welfare but for her mother and father's. She had mentioned how stressed her mom was about her dad, but she didn't tell Derrick if the problems were personal or political."

"Interesting. Okay, what's your next step?"

Renz took over. "We're heading back to our office to begin looking into Michael Kent's background to see if there's ever been grievances filed against him and, if so, by whom. Political issues would be news fodder and publicized, but if there were personal improprieties, they may be harder to dig up. There's always the chance that he's being blackmailed, and maybe that's why Marie is stressed. The other murders are connected, and as soon as we figure out how, we'll be able to follow the bread crumbs to the root cause."

"Good. We need to nip this in the bud and fast. The mayor has his own security detail and lives in a walled and gated compound, but as far as the families of the other victims are concerned, and because we don't know the connection yet, they're kind of on their own."

I had to agree, although people generally took extra precautions when tragic events affected their lives.

Renz and I settled in at our desks and got busy reviewing archived newspaper and internet articles. We wrote down the names of anyone who came up as having a beef with the city administration or the mayor.

After an hour of digging, I stood, stretched, and grabbed a couple of bucks out of my purse. "Want a soda?"

"Yeah, thanks." Renz looked at me and tapped his pen against his desk as if it helped him think.

"For God's sake, just say what's on your mind."

"This doesn't feel right."

I sat back down. "In what way?"

"We aren't going to find the connection like this. That's telling me this isn't a political matter because the victims didn't have a political connection to the mayor."

"Right, but someone in their six degrees might have."

"Let's wait for everyone to get back with their results. We've already spent an hour that I think was a waste of time."

"So in the meantime?"

Renz's phone rang, and he raised his hand. "Hold that thought." He lifted the receiver from the base and answered the call. "DeLeon speaking. Yeah, we're on our way."

"What's going on? Something good, I hope."

"Not sure, but Taft wants us back in her office right away."

We charged down the hall to our boss's office, and she waved us in before Renz had a chance to knock.

"What's up, Boss?"

"You two spent more time with Erik Smalley than anyone else, right?"

"Right," I said.

"Okay. I was just sent this grainy video from District Six, and it shows somebody leaving the alley in the time frame of Brandon's murder. What I need to know, since the footage is from a half block away, is if you think that person is Erik Smalley." She waved us to her side of the desk. "Give it careful consideration and don't say yes just because it would fit the narrative. Take your time."

Renz scooted the roller chairs closer, and Taft moved out of our way. We had seen Erik on the bank's video and had watched it numerous times. The man leaving the alley wore a windbreaker like Erik did on Saturday, and his hair was black like Erik's. I studied his mannerisms and gait. He looked down as he walked and had a long stride.

I voiced my opinion. "I think it's him."

Taft looked at Renz. "Lorenzo?"

"I agree. That search warrant is still good on Erik's apartment and belongings, right?"

Taft said that it was.

"But nothing of importance was found there," I said.

Renz palmed his forehead. "If you recall, Erik didn't seem all that nervous when I said our agents were already going through his apartment. That's because if he was the shooter, he'd already offloaded the gun. The only evidence was that windbreaker he grabbed when we hauled him in for questioning. His smug self thought we wouldn't find a video of him leaving the alley that showed he had on the same jacket he wore Saturday. The agents searched the duplex and found nothing because their focus was on the gun. We should have ripped that jacket off Erik's body during his interview and had it tested for GSR, but we were only thinking of the gun. If we're going to prove that Erik is the shooter, then we need that jacket."

I groaned. "If it's not too late. He may have washed it already."

"Or maybe not. Narcissistic people who think they're smarter than the cops tend to let their guard down. We need to pay him another visit and grab that jacket."

Taft jerked her head toward the door. "Go ahead and do it now."

We returned to Erik's West Allis apartment and banged on the door. We knew somebody was there since the lights were on and sounds were coming from inside. They likely thought we'd just go away if they didn't answer.

Renz pounded harder the second time and yelled Erik's name. We were ignored.

"Looks like the door is going down."

"I'll give them one more chance, and then I'm kicking it in." Renz yelled that we still had a warrant and if somebody didn't open the door immediately, it would be kicked down. A grin spread across his face when we heard footsteps running down the stairs.

"All right, already. Damn cops just don't stop, do you?"

We pushed our way past Cole, the other roommate, as he opened the door. "We aren't cops, and where is Erik?"

"He isn't here."

Renz and I continued up the stairs then searched every room. Cole was right—Erik wasn't there.

"Where did he go?" I asked.

Cole shrugged. "Who knows? I'm not his mommy."

I glared at him. "That's the best you've got? Which room is Erik's?"

The kid tipped his head to the right. "The messiest one—over there."

I walked in, looked around, and saw the windbreaker lying on the floor at the foot of the bed. I pulled my phone from my pocket, took several pictures of the jacket, then slipped on my gloves and picked it up. I took several more pictures, gave it a once-over, and walked out of the room with it. I handed my phone to Renz and stood next to Cole with the jacket held up. "Take a few more pictures, Renz, so nobody can deny this jacket came from this residence."

"Smart thinking, Jade." Renz took the pictures with Cole in the frame. "Okay, we have what we came for. Let's go."

Before returning to our headquarters, we dropped off the jacket at the county crime lab and told them we needed it tested for GSR as soon as possible. Hal said he would call with the results in a few hours. Time was of the essence, and if any residue remained on the jacket after a full day, it would be tiny particles, but between that and the alley video, we would have all we needed to arrest Erik Smalley for murder.

Chapter 31

I knew we were in for a long night and couldn't imagine getting home before ten o'clock. The time didn't matter. I was excited to learn what the other agents had found out after pressing the people they'd interviewed earlier about possible connections to the mayor.

We gathered around the conference room table. Taft tipped her head at Kyle, likely because he and Charlotte were to her left.

Charlotte nodded to her partner. "Go ahead, Kyle. You can start the ball rolling."

"Sure." He let out a puff of air and began. "We interviewed Pete Lawrence's widow again and asked more about the twin, Paul, since he was too distraught to speak with us earlier. She gave us details about his profession and said that he wasn't an ordinary bartender but one of those charismatic types who excelled at flamboyant tricks with drinks, glasses, and bottles."

I frowned. "That's a thing? Like in that eighties movie?"

"I guess so, but here's the real kicker. Paul Lawrence is a freelance bartender and works a lot of fundraising and charity events. Those types of events would be something the mayor would obviously attend."

Taft wrote that down. "That's interesting. Okay, so what have you got, Carl?"

"After speaking with Sheila Kam's daughter for the second time, we learned that she goes by her maiden name, Rebecca Kam. Her high-profile-attorney husband is Douglas Blake."

Taft nodded. "I've heard the name."

"Right. It took a lot of digging into the archives, but we found out that he's the mayor's personal attorney. He's represented Michael Kent through the years with estate taxes, wills, settlements, benefactors, endowments, and the like, especially when his grandparents and more recently his own parents passed. Some disgruntled cousin contested Michael's father's will, saying that his own father, Michael's brother, Ted, who had squandered his inheritance from the grandparents, deserved more money."

"So there was bad blood between an uncle, a cousin, and Michael?" I asked.

"Possibly, and we can check for alibis, but that's a solid connection leading directly to the mayor."

It certainly is," Taft said. "Tommy and Fay, did you learn anything new from Amanda's parents?"

"They own Silver Shores Resort, and since we've now learned that Paul Lawrence freelances his bartending services, that could be a connection. We already know from their website that Silver Shores hosts banquets and charity events on a regular basis. We'll make the call and ask if they've ever hired Paul Lawrence and if the mayor had ever attended an event there when Mr. Lawrence bartended."

My enthusiasm was building. "We're definitely getting somewhere."

"What about George Patrick? Was there more information brought to light about him?"

Charlotte took her turn. "We spoke with most of his neighbors earlier except the person who lived right next door on his left. Nobody answered our knock when we were there before. When we returned a few hours ago, we saw a car in the driveway, so we went to the door. A midforties looking woman answered. We told her who we were and said we'd been there earlier but nobody was home. She introduced herself as Julie Beckett and told us she had just gotten home from work. After inviting us in, she talked about George, and from the look on her face, it was obvious that she cared deeply for him. She said she'd lived in her home for thirteen years, and George was not only her go-to guy who fixed everything for her but her dearest friend. She said life would never be the same without him, and if there hadn't been a crisis that forced her to be at her workplace, she would have taken a few days off."

Kyle took over. "That's when I asked her where she worked, and she said city hall. I'm sure our hearts skipped a beat when she said that, and then I pressed harder by asking her in what capacity." Kyle looked at each of us. "Ready for this?"

I swatted the air. "Well, yeah. Let's hear it."

"She's the mayor's personal assistant."

That was the first time I'd ever heard Taft curse. We all stared silently at her and waited. It took a few seconds, then she glanced at the wall clock. "When are we going to get the GSR results?"

"We were told it'll take a few hours, Maureen," Renz said. "Meanwhile, we can put those puzzle pieces together like we talked about."

We hadn't mentioned seeing the bottle of bourbon on the mayor's library desk at ten that morning or when we'd returned a few hours later and he was three sheets to the wind. People coped with tragedy and mourned in different ways, and I assumed the drinking was his way to numb the pain or possibly the guilt. I couldn't fault him since I didn't know the man personally and had no idea if his wife, closest friends, and workmates were covering up for him drinking too much.

Renz began the puzzle. "Okay, we have Silver Shores Resort that hosts charity functions and fundraising events. The daughter of owners Roger and Tina Kennedy, Amanda, was murdered. They possibly hired Paul Lawrence to bartend there on a night that hosted an event the mayor might have been at. Both very possible scenarios, and we can easily find out that information with a phone call. Paul's brother, Pete, was murdered. Then we have Douglas Blake, the personal attorney for the mayor, and his mother-in-law, Sheila Kam, was murdered. Finally, there's Julie Beckett, who happens to be the mayor's personal assistant, and George Patrick, a factory foreman, her neighbor, and best friend, was murdered. To me, it sounds like the killers want to inflict pain on the mayor and the people affiliated with him."

"And once we find out the why, we'll also know the who," I said as I gave Renz a slight head tip.

"I saw that," Tommy said. "What gives?"

I groaned. "We did notice a bottle of bourbon on the mayor's desk this morning, and then when we went back to question him later, he was completely incoherent. We didn't have the opportunity to speak with him at all, and the wife was less than inviting and asked us to leave. She said if we wanted to speak to her husband again, we'd have to give them a twenty-four hour notice."

"That seems more than telling," Taft said. She turned to Tommy. "Pull up the mayor's name on the county arrest database. See if he's ever been hauled in for public intoxication, public disturbances, speeding, drunk driving or driving recklessly, and so on. Run the gamut on him."

"Roger that."

"Meanwhile, have the BOLOs hit on any of the missing vehicles?" Fay asked.

Maureen said two more cars had been located at homes of known felons. "I imagine the cars were abandoned with the keys inside and it didn't take long for opportunistic crooks to lay claim to them. Those cars have been taken to the crime lab's garage and will be gone over from top to bottom. That leaves two more cars to track down, yet as slow as it seems, we are making progress."

When my phone buzzed on the table, everyone looked my way. "That has to be the crime lab with the GSR results," I said.

Taft jerked her chin toward me. "Put it on Speaker."

I answered my phone then tapped the speaker icon. "Agent Monroe here."

"Agent Monroe, it's Hal from the crime lab. We have the results on the GSR."

"Yes, and?"

"We found traces, slight ones, but traces nonetheless."

I fist-pumped the air, and Taft took over.

"Hal, it's Supervisory Special Agent Taft speaking."

"Yes, ma'am."

"Is there enough GSR present to make an arrest? No question?"

"No question, ma'am. If there isn't a logical explanation for GSR to be on the sleeves of that jacket, then an arrest is definitely in order."

"Thanks, Hal. We'll need that jacket secured and the report sent over to Agent Monroe's email immediately. Great work."

"Thank you, and I'll send the report right now."

I ended the call, and our entire group let out relieved yelps.

Taft lifted the receiver from the conference room phone and called the West Allis PD. She asked them to pick up Erik Smalley at his residence immediately, and if he wasn't there, to put out an APB on him. He would be charged with the murder of Brandon Dalton.

I rattled my fingertips on the table. "Okay, so we assume Erik killed Brandon, but why? The only thing I can think of is that Brandon went back to the tent city because he dropped something the night before and was looking for it. Erik might have seen him purely by accident once Brandon was walking Hemmer Street, or he was following Brandon, saw that he returned to the scene of the crime, and was given the order to take him out. It would sure be nice to find that gun."

Taft frowned. "Erik doesn't have any firearms registered to him, correct?"

"That's correct," Renz said.

"So he borrowed a gun, or was given a gun to commit the murder, and then returned it to the person he got it from. That person may be literally calling the shots."

"And I'd put my money on both Brandon and Erik as two of the killers of the homeless people," I said.

Maureen agreed. "And there's a good chance that Erik is one of them who took part in killing the five people last night."

"Hmm... there's still a missing piece to the puzzle," I said.

"Go on."

I nodded at our boss. "We know who was killed and the whole six-degree thing that leads back to the mayor, but two of those five people don't actually have any affiliation with Michael Kent at all. Only his daughter, his personal assistant, and his attorney have a direct connection to him. The owners of Silver Shores and the bartender who *might* have worked there during a charity event that the mayor *might* have been at, likely don't know Michael Kent on a personal level at all. So how do they fit in?"

"Good question, and instead of speculating, we need to know definitively if there was an event that the mayor went to and if Paul Lawrence bartended that night." Maureen turned to Tommy. "Since you and Fay spoke with Mr. and Mrs. Kennedy, make that call, have them pull the records or connect you with whoever handles scheduling those events, and find out the date that the mayor and Paul Lawrence were there at the same time, if they ever were. Everyone else, take a ten-minute break." Maureen rose from the table and walked to the door. "I'll start a pot of coffee."

Chapter 32

While I took my break, I called Amber to tell her not to expect me home anytime soon. I would be fine with a warmed-up plate of leftovers later. We gathered in the conference room at eight thirty and waited for the results to come in from Tommy, who was still on the phone.

Maureen poured coffee into nine cups, and we all helped ourselves. Seconds later, her phone rang. She listened, spoke, then hung up and passed on the information. The West Allis PD said they hadn't located Erik Smalley, but an APB had been put out on him.

"It's going to be tough finding him since he doesn't have a vehicle on file, and when a vehicle is necessary, they just steal one. A weasel like him can scurry in and out of the shadows easily, especially if he suspects somebody is tailing him." Something popped into my head as soon as the words came out of my mouth. "We need to locate the closest bus stops to his house and put down anchors. It's the best way to find him."

"I agree," Maureen said, "and—"

Tommy hung up and interrupted Maureen midsentence.

"We have the connection! There was a fundraiser held on the fifth of May at Silver Shores for the new firehouse on the northeast side. The mayor was the guest of honor at the function, and the celebrity bartender was none other than Paul Lawrence."

"Okay, you two need to rattle his cage right now. I know he's distraught, but so are all the other families, and we have to find out what happened between them that night."

I gulped down my coffee with intentions of leaving too. I had a suggestion to run by Taft, and I hoped she would okay it. "Maureen, back to the bus-shelter idea. I just looked on my phone, and there are two of them within three blocks of the duplex Erik lives in. Brandon spoke of taking the bus, but then they both ended up in a stolen car. I'm figuring that's how most of them get around, either by bus or stolen vehicles. Just a few more ways to keep under the radar and make tracking them down hard on the cops. I'll be heading north to go home anyway. I can sit on one of those shelters, and as long as they stay out of sight, a squad car can sit on the other. I know what Erik looks like, and in my personal car, I can get pretty close without raising a red flag."

She rubbed her forehead. "I don't like the idea of you taking on that responsibility alone."

"I won't be alone. I'll have the West Allis PD sitting on the other shelter only a few blocks away. I can let them know if I spot Erik, and if it makes you feel better, I'll have them assist in the arrest."

"Okay, let's go that route. I'd really like to have that punk in custody tonight."

"Hold up," Renz said. "Why would Erik go back home? Don't you think Lucas or Cole would have told him we were there earlier and took his windbreaker, and then the cops showed up later? Home is the last place he'd go, and that's likely why he wasn't there when the cops came back to arrest him."

Renz had a point, and Erik Smalley was either roaming the streets or bunking up somewhere else, and we had no idea where that place might be.

"Then what about following the roommates?" I asked. "They could be party to all of this since they have the same police records that Erik does. Just because the charges were for rioting doesn't mean they aren't real criminals. Now that we have justifiable cause to follow Erik, there's a good chance his roommates may lead us right to him."

"That could work. I'll have the PD bang on the door again to verify that at least one of them is at home. You can sit on the house, Jade, and if anything, they'll be watching for a squad car planted outside. They won't even notice you if they do leave."

"Right, and if they hop on a bus, I'll be right behind it until they get off. I'll have whatever police district I'm in assist in following them once they're on foot. They'll lead us to either Erik or somebody else who might be part of that group. No matter what, somebody is going to do some talking tonight."

Taft finally agreed. "Okay, that sounds like a plan. The rest of you start searching archives to see if anything newsworthy went down on that night last May."

Chapter 33

Two officers met me around the corner from Erik Smalley's apartment to go over the plan. They would wait for me to get into position with a good view of the duplex, then they'd park in front of it and bang on the door for the second time in several hours. We were setting a trap that I hoped would pan out. If it didn't, Erik Smalley's face would be plastered on every news channel until someone from his group gave him up or he was spotted and turned in by a concerned citizen.

As a precaution, I exchanged cell phone numbers with the officers. Nothing about what we were doing would be broadcast over the police radios. For all we knew, the people who were involved in the murders could have scanners.

I found a good place across the street to park, cut the engine and lights, and let the officers know I was ready whenever they were.

A minute later, I saw headlights coming my way through the rearview mirror. The squad car passed me then parked in plain view of the upper unit's front window. From my position, I saw lights on upstairs. I watched as the officers approached the duplex, walked the sidewalk to the porch, then banged on the door to the upstairs apartment. A man came to the window and looked down. There was no denying that at least one person was home. After the officers waited on the porch for several minutes, the door swung open, and they disappeared inside.

I made the call to Taft and updated her on where I was and what I was watching. I told her I'd keep her posted and hung up. Even though I knew I was on Speakerphone and Renz was listening in, I planned to call his cell and update him, too, every half hour or so.

My hope was that the roommates would leave as soon as they saw the police car drive away. Sometimes a little prodding went a long way, and I crossed my fingers that they'd take the bait and leave. That was when the real investigation would begin. There was a good chance that they knew where Erik was and who the puppet masters were, and hopefully, they'd lead us right to them.

Ten minutes later, the cops exited the building, climbed into their squad car, and drove off. That same man came to the window again and looked out. I called Officer Brice to tell him that they had been seen driving away. "Are they both up there?"

"Yep, both Lucas and Cole are home."

"Okay."

If the roommates were going anywhere, it would probably be in the next few minutes. While I watched the duplex, I wondered how Erik had gotten to the alley, was in the car with Brandon, yet never showed up on any cameras near his home between seven and eight a.m. that Sunday morning.

Maybe he left even earlier than that or stayed the night somewhere else, yet there is the chance he sneaked out using the fire escape and jumped the fence, but why sneak out at all? That's just one more puzzle piece we need to figure out. No matter what, he's good for the murder. Now all we need to do is track him down.

As I stared at the duplex, the upstairs lights went off. "Yes!" I realized I was holding my breath as I watched the front door. A minute later, I saw movement. The door opened slightly. A head popped out and looked up and down the street, then cautiously, both men walked out. I kept low in my seat but still had a good visual of them. They turned right and hurried down the sidewalk. As they walked away from me, I sat up and made another call to Officer Brice. I told him that both men were on foot, walking east down Greenfield Avenue, and would probably pass them as they sat on the next side street within a minute or two. If the guys planned to hop on a bus, they were headed in the right direction. The nearest bus stop was only two blocks away.

I started my car and inched ahead. I didn't want to get too close, but I didn't want to lose them either. I made sure to cut in and out of the commercial driveways so they wouldn't notice a car following them at a slow pace. They were coming up on the bus shelter, so I turned in at a gas station and waited. Brice called my phone and asked my location. I told them where I was, and he said they had passed the shelter on a parallel street and were stationed a half block ahead with a clear view of both men. They had just taken seats in the enclosure and were waiting for the next bus. Brice said that this particular bus went due east and ended at South Barclay Street just blocks from Jones Island. There was nothing in that area except derelict homes, abandoned warehouses, and homeless people, which could be exactly what we were looking for.

I looked to my left, and the city bus was approaching. Cole, Lucas, and one woman were waiting in the shelter. After the bus stopped and the riders exited, both men and the woman climbed aboard. Brice and I were still on the phone, and he reminded me that they could assist the entire way since West Allis and Barclay Street were both part of the second district jurisdiction. I was glad that I wouldn't have to ask for different officers from another precinct and explain the situation to them. Brice said they would update the precincts on their end and he'd make the call with his cell.

It took twenty-five minutes to reach the end of the bus route, but Lucas and Cole had already gotten off at the First Street stop. I didn't like the idea that I was completely exposed even though I was in my personal car. The area was desolate, and a car following, even at a distance, would probably raise a red flag. I had to back off, park, and follow them on foot. It was the only way, or I'd lose them for sure. I called Brice, told him my plan, and turned down a side street. The squad car was only a few car lengths behind me. After I exited my vehicle and peered around a building, I saw the men walk north. Brice and Connelly parked behind my car and came my way.

"What have we got?" Connelly asked.

"They're right there." I pointed at the men a good block ahead. "The only way to get close enough to see where they're going is on foot, but we'll need to split up. I'll go straight up the middle, Brice, you go a half block to their left, and Connelly, you go a half block to their right. As long as one of us has a visual on them at all times, we'll be able to see where they went. Set your phones to vibrate, I'll do the same, and we'll keep each other posted via texts. Any questions?"

"Nope, I'm good," Brice said.

Connelly nodded. "Me too."

The officers scurried off in opposite directions. I lost sight of them as they rounded the buildings, then I sucked in a deep breath and moved ahead cautiously.

Chapter 34

I still had the guys in my sights and moved in even closer while I hugged the brick walls. As I deliberately stayed in the shadows, the phone in my pocket vibrated, momentarily distracting me.

"Damn it." I checked the screen, and it was Renz. I shouldn't have, but I answered anyway and whispered. "I can't talk right now. I'm following Cole and Lucas on foot. Yeah, yeah, the cops are with me, but we split up, each a half block from the other. We have our phones to keep in touch and don't intend to apprehend them until we're all together again. We just need to see where they go. I have to hang up now." I ended the call, pocketed my phone, rounded the corner of the building, and was instantly clocked in the face hard enough to knock me off my feet. Stars swirled in my head as I stumbled backward and fell to the ground, but it took only a second to regain my bearings and right myself. I pulled out my gun and peeked around the corner. Nobody was in sight, but I heard the sound of running in the distance. I could either make a foot pursuit or take the time to call the officers, but doing that meant holstering my gun to pull out my phone and dial. Carefully, I looked around the building and saw a flash of movement when someone turned the corner a block up the street. I holstered my weapon and made the call. "Brice, somebody just cold-cocked me, but I'm okay. I saw a person about a block north of my location, but they disappeared around a corner. Be ready for anything and be careful. I'm continuing on." I hung up, pulled my Glock out again, and headed in the direction where I last saw the person.

The streetlights were few and far between, which didn't help in our pursuit, but the lack of light helped us stay hidden. I must have been discovered during my short conversation with Renz. I had known better than to pick up, but I did anyway, and somebody, either Cole or Lucas, had heard my whispers and backtracked to my location. That told me they were as brazen and dangerous as Erik, and even though they were young, they were still a threat. I had to keep in mind that they didn't hesitate to knock me— a federal agent—for a loop, and killing everyday citizens probably didn't faze them either.

My eyes darted left and right as I searched the darkness in hopes of seeing more movement, but I didn't. Connelly and Brice met up with me minutes later.

"Anything?" I asked.

They both said they'd lost the guys as they weaved in and out of alleyways and around vacant warehouses.

"Do you think they entered one of these buildings, or did they just use them to lose us in the darkness? They may have moved farther north where there's actually a few houses," I said.

Connelly pulled his flashlight from his pocket. "Close your eyes."

I did as told while he assessed my facial injury.

"Yeah, you got clobbered good, and your nose is swelling up. Can you breathe okay?"

I swatted the air. "I'll be fine. I'm just pissed that we lost them. Maybe we should check out the buildings anyway since we all have flashlights and those punks already know we're here."

"The problem is, we have no idea how many of them there are and, if they're still here, what building they might be in." Connelly took in our surroundings. "It's damn dark outside, and you'd think if they went into a building, they'd need a light source. I'd suggest we stay out here but walk past the buildings. If anybody is inside, we'd likely see a bit of light, but in the dark like this, it's too dangerous to pursue them since we don't know if they're armed or not. They could have those knives or garrotes with them— maybe even guns."

Brice agreed. "But if you want, we could call for backup and go through all of these vacant warehouses."

I groaned. "I'm sure if we got close, they'd scatter. Going through these buildings is probably wiser during daylight hours. We don't know if the structures are even safe to enter. There is one thing I do know."

"Yeah, what's that?" Brice asked.

"There's a reason those two came here. That tent city south of downtown and under the overpass is very similar to this area, with abandoned warehouses and factories. This type of place could be where the killers meet to make their plans. No normal citizen hangs out there, and the homeless aren't going to question why they're in the area. They'd probably be afraid to make waves."

Brice huffed. "And maybe seeing those homeless people prompted the idea of using them for their practice murders."

I knew Brice was on to something, and I needed to get Taft's opinion on whether we should search the buildings, get more officers out to help, or leave it to the safer daylight hours.

"Let me talk to my supervisor and see what she wants us to do." I made the call, and Taft said not to pursue, especially after I told her I'd been sucker punched. She said she would have the police departments send officers out there tomorrow when daylight made everything safer. She told me to thank the officers, go home, and get some sleep. An APB would go out for Cole Pratt and Lucas Freeman, too, and she'd have their duplex under constant surveillance beginning that night. Tomorrow, the faces of Erik, Lucas, and Cole would be broadcast on every news station. We would close in, force them out of hiding, and make the arrests. They'd give us the names of the people who were calling the shots, or all three would face murder charges as well as battery charges on a federal agent.

Chapter 35

Cole and Lucas put enough distance between themselves and that bitch FBI agent that there was time to warn the others. The group left silently and scattered in different directions, with instructions from Jacob and Evelyn to reconvene tomorrow at noon at the original site, where they would learn who the final targets were. Even though Jacob and Evelyn wanted to enjoy committing those last murders themselves, they would have backup along in case something went sideways.

They thanked Cole and Lucas for their quick thinking then left.

Erik, Cole, and Lucas headed north on foot with no place in mind. They couldn't return to the duplex since they realized too late that they'd been duped. That woman agent had to have been outside and followed them when they left the building.

"Why didn't you just stay home?" Erik asked. "Now they know where that location is, meaning we can't go back there again."

"We went because Jacob said to meet there at ten

o'clock. I didn't really want to get on his bad side by being a no-show," Cole said. "We didn't know we were being followed until we got off the bus. We saw headlights a half block behind us, continued on, but then circled back when we heard footsteps getting closer. I heard someone talking on their phone, too, and it turned out to be that same agent who thought she was hot shit by having her partner take a picture of me and her together as proof that your windbreaker came from the apartment."

"And then they took it?"

"That's exactly what they did."

Erik paced. "We need somewhere to stay since I'm sure the apartment is being watched."

"Let's head to the underpass where Brandon offed that homeless woman. It's close to the warehouse, and then tomorrow, we'll ask about staying with someone from the group. Jacob will make one of the recruits put us up," Lucas said.

"We better hope so, or we'll be living alongside those homeless assholes under the overpass." Erik jerked his head. "Come on. Let's continue north for a few blocks and then catch a bus."

Chapter 36

Sleep didn't come easily that night even with a melatonin tablet and four aspirin. I knew we were close to our aha moment, and I couldn't wait to find out if our gut instincts were right. Did all of those murders lead right back to the mayor, and if so, why? If we found something horrific that happened in May on the same night the mayor attended the function at Silver Shores Resort and Paul Lawrence was bartending, we could possibly piece together a motive for the murders. Somehow, some way, Michael Kent was the catalyst.

I had to force myself out of bed that Tuesday morning, not because I wasn't excited to get to work but because I was still exhausted. I stumbled into the bathroom and took a look at my face in the mirror. I groaned. "You've got to be kidding." My nose was swollen, and hints of blue underlined both eyes. I let out a puff of air and turned on the shower faucet. "What else is new?"

After taking a hot shower and getting dressed, I downed two cups of coffee and a filling egg-and-bacon breakfast, compliments of my little sister. Then I was back in form and raring to go. I listened as Amber berated me about being more careful. I thanked her for the concern then heard the same warning from Kate when she entered the kitchen.

"What the hell happened to you?"

"I slammed into a fist last night."

She shook her head. "Or a fist slammed into you. You really ought to be more careful. It isn't like you're a rookie cop for Pete's sake."

"Sorry. I was on the phone with Renz when some asshat sucker punched me in the dark just as I hung up. I didn't see or hear him coming." I guzzled the last of my coffee. "Gotta go. Maybe if we're lucky, we'll capture those punks and get them to talk."

"Is one of those punks the asshat who clocked you?" Kate asked.

"Yep, he sure is."

"Good, then I hope you get them too."

I said my goodbyes and headed out. I couldn't wait to hear if any of those three had been apprehended overnight. If they hadn't been, we would air all their faces on the news and do our best to put them behind bars before the end of the day. Tommy and Fay should have news to share about their interview with Paul Lawrence last night, and then as a team, we needed to search harder in the archived records for something that might have happened in May to set the killing spree in motion. The problem was, we had no idea what we were searching for.

I made it through a traffic slowdown on I-43 as I

traveled south but still arrived at work on time. Hopefully, that was the sign of a good day to come. I was about to climb the three flights of stairs as my morning workout when I saw Renz standing at the elevator. I decided to join him instead.

"I guess you don't know any more than I do since you're just getting here too."

Renz stared at my bruised face. "Wow."

I held up my hand. "I don't need a third scolding. I've already gotten enough from Amber and Kate."

"And rightfully so."

I huffed and pointed at my nose. "This is actually your fault for calling me last night."

"Or your fault for answering."

"One could argue that point too." I chuckled and pressed the button for the third floor. "Hopefully, Tommy and Fay got something from Paul Lawrence that'll help."

Renz shook his head as if in doubt. "Why would a bartender have any kind of altercation with the mayor, though? I'm sure security people were there as well, and they'd run interference if something took place between them."

The elevator's ding indicated that we'd arrived on the third floor. The steel box bounced slightly then stopped, and the doors parted. We made a quick detour at our office to drop off our jackets then headed down the hallway to see if everyone was there. I was excited to get our morning updates underway and to find out if Taft had heard of any new developments since she'd arrived. Maureen waved us in then sighed when she saw my face. I assured her I was fine.

"We'll begin in ten minutes since we're still waiting on Kyle to show up. I, for one, am excited to hear about Tommy's conversation with Paul Lawrence," she said.

It was my turn to make the coffee, and I had just enough time to brew a pot and set the carafe on the table before everyone filed into the room. We took our seats, Taft said none of the guys had been apprehended during the night, then she opened the meeting with a head tip at Tommy.

"Go ahead and tell us what you learned from Paul Lawrence. We're all sitting on pins and needles."

Tommy blew out a long breath. I took that to mean he didn't have earth-shattering news to share, and I felt my shoulders slump.

"Well, I'll admit I felt really bad for the guy. He was truly suffering from the loss of his twin brother, and I'm sure *his* focus wasn't even on the questions we asked. He seemed annoyed that *our* focus was on Michael Kent instead of his brother's murder."

Fay spoke up. "But who could blame him? The FBI comes to talk to him and he probably thought we had news about the killer. Instead, we ask questions about a night he bartended at Silver Shores during a fundraiser when the mayor happened to be there. To top it off, that was five months ago. He looked at us like we were crazy."

Taft nodded for Fay to continue. "And then what?"

Fay sighed. "And then not much. He said he barely remembered that night other than the fact that the mayor was there. Paul went on to say that the mayor gave a short speech about the fundraiser, schmoozed with people, and then planted his ass at the bar for several hours. He couldn't recall anything out of the ordinary as far as the mayor was concerned. Paul said he had to cut people off throughout the night, as he always did, and the mayor was one of them. Paul couldn't recall how many glasses of bourbon the mayor had, but he did remember the mayor being pissed when Paul eventually closed his tab. He said the fundraiser was over with anyway, and the resort was clearing out. He admitted that he should have cut off the mayor long before that, but since he was the guest of honor, he didn't want to make waves."

"Humph. That doesn't sound any different than what most bartenders do when it's necessary," I said.

"So there wasn't an altercation between them?" Taft asked.

Tommy took over. "It didn't sound like anything that would attract attention and embarrass the mayor."

Taft tapped the table. "Unfortunately, people can be at the same event and remember things differently. Somebody had to be angry enough with Paul Lawrence to kill his brother, and we know it isn't the mayor who's doing the killings since his own daughter was murdered." Taft tipped her head at Tommy. "Get more names of people who were at that event. I want to hear other eyewitness accounts from people who were at the bar when the mayor was. I want to know just how drunk he was before Paul Lawrence cut him off and if there were heated words between them or possibly threats too."

Chapter 37

If anyone other than the eyewitnesses at the May event knew what had gone down that night, it could be the mayor's personal assistant or his attorney. There was a chance that the assistant had spoken with Mr. and Mrs. Kennedy or the function coordinator and arranged for the mayor to make an appearance and a speech at the fundraiser. His showing up would definitely increase attendance and help fund the new fire station being built at that time.

I passed my suggestion on to Taft, and she said to go ahead and make the call. I also mentioned that if something involving Paul Lawrence and the mayor did occur at the event, there was a chance that the attorney had been briefed about it. I would call him, too, and request records of phone calls or appointments between him and the mayor over the last six months. Chances were he'd deny us access and a warrant would have to be issued.

Renz and I returned to our office and settled in. He would call Douglas Blake, the attorney, and I would contact the mayor's assistant, Julie Beckett.

We knew the mayor was taking the week off because of

his daughter's death and that the deputy mayor, John Branford, was filling in for him. The funeral service for Tamara Kent wouldn't take place until Saturday, when all of the city employees could attend. Meanwhile, for the rest of the week, Julie Beckett was reporting directly to John Branford.

After dialing city hall and going through five prompts before I got to the mayor's office, I finally reached the automated assistant who asked for the name of the party or extension I wanted to reach. I said the name Julie Beckett since I didn't know her extension. I waited as the phone rang in my ear three times before it connected to a voice. My excitement faded quickly when I realized it was only a voicemail greeting. Disappointed, I left a message and hung up. Most requests for a return call went without a reply. I'd always assumed that people weren't curious enough to return a call to the FBI, and whether that was from fear, guilt, or the thought that they were being pranked, most people didn't want to talk to us, and that meant more work in chasing them down. I set my phone timer to remind me to try again in thirty minutes.

From the phone conversation Renz was having, it didn't sound like the attorney was too excited about handing over phone records or his appointment calendar. I heard Renz use the word *warrant* more than once before he hung up.

I groaned in frustration after he placed the receiver on the base. "No luck either?"

"Nah, he's playing hardball with me, but that's okay. I know how this back-and-forth thing works, but in the meantime, we'll ask for the warrant anyway. No skin off my back, and he knows it. He either gives me what I asked for, or the warrant will cover anything and everything we want to look at. Doubt if he wants that to happen." Renz glanced at the clock. "I bet I'll get a callback in less than an hour."

"And the warrant?"

"I'll let Taft know we need one." Renz picked up the receiver again and dialed our boss.

He set the phone to Speaker, and I listened as they talked. Taft said she'd had enough. The APBs were taking too long, and she was ready to post all three faces and descriptions on the news channels. Anyone affiliated with Erik, Lucas, or Cole would likely go underground, which would make finding the ringleader tougher, but if we captured any of those three, we would convince them to talk one way or another. The cards were stacked against them, especially Erik since we had proof of his murdering Brandon thanks to the GSR evidence on his jacket. Cole was also looking at plenty of time behind bars for slugging me in the face. Taft said the TV stations agreed to run their mug shots and descriptions on the air—every hour on the hour—as breaking news. Some concerned citizen would see them, do the right thing, be in the limelight momentarily, and enjoy their fifteen minutes of fame—I hoped.

I looked at the timer on my phone again. Still seventeen minutes to go.

"What about the Kam brother, Jeremy? Isn't he supposed to arrive from New Mexico today?"

Renz said he was, but he didn't know when. During his

conversation with Renz, Douglas Blake hadn't mentioned his brother-in-law, or when Jeremy was scheduled to arrive in Milwaukee, at all.

George Patrick's mom and dad were flying in from Florida, and they still needed to be talked to. Chloe, Brandon's sister, was also on my mind, but she'd said they weren't close. Because she lived halfway across the country and was married and seven years older, I didn't much hope that she knew anything about Brandon's acquaintances. We were running out of people who could give us information that we didn't already have.

My phone's buzzer sounded, and I made the second call to Julie Beckett. That time, she picked up, and I fist-pumped the air. Renz gave me a reassuring glance and a thumbs-up. I was stoked, and there was no way I would let her slip out of answering my questions. If we had to issue warrants for every person the mayor knew and every document that might give us the answers we needed, then so be it. I began as soon as she said hello.

"Ms. Beckett?"

"Yes, this is she. Who's calling?"

"This is SSA Jade Monroe from the FBI's serial crimes unit."

"Serial crimes? Are you sure you're calling the right person?"

"I'm more than sure, ma'am."

"Please don't call me ma'am. I'm not that old. So what can I do for you, Agent Monroe?"

"I'm calling about the fundraiser that took place at Silver

Shores Resort in May. It was a benefit and silent auction to raise money for the new firehouse on the east side."

"Yes, I recall that fundraiser. What about it?"

"If I'm not mistaken, the mayor attended that event. Did you set that up?"

"No, I'm not his PR person. I don't set up his calendar of appearances."

Her response took me by surprise, and I wasn't quite sure what to ask next.

"Is that it? I'm rather busy."

Her tone irritated me, and I couldn't understand why she was trying to get me off the phone. "Actually, no, that isn't it. You were aware that the mayor attended that event, even if you aren't his PR person. Am I correct?"

She huffed into the phone. "If you had any idea how many functions the mayor attends every year, you wouldn't ask that question."

"Well, I did, and I'd like an answer." I went quiet and waited. Silence filled her end of the line for a good fifteen seconds before she spoke.

"I'm aware he attended that event."

"Good, and what kind of records are kept for every function the mayor goes to?"

"I couldn't say. Like I told you before, I'm not his PR person."

"Then I'll need the name of the person who is."

She huffed again, and for whatever reason, I seemed to be getting on her nerves. "His name is Noah Cummings. Now if—"

I interrupted before she had the chance to hang up on me. "One more thing."

She groaned. "What is it?"

"Since you're his personal assistant, what exactly are the duties you perform for the mayor?"

"Emergency services, errands, and cleaning up messes. Things that go beyond his daily role as mayor."

"Cleaning up messes? Would you care to expand on that?"

"No. Now I really have to go."

The phone clicked in my ear, and the line went dead. "Wow."

Renz frowned. "Want to explain *wow* to me?"

I shook my head. "I guess I'd envisioned Julie Beckett as a sweet, heartfelt human being when Charlotte and Kyle described their interview with her."

"And she isn't?"

I pulled back. "Not from the conversation we just had. She strikes me more as having a pit bull personality."

"That's odd."

I raised my brows. "Get this. She said one of her roles was to clean up the mayor's messes."

Now it was Renz's turn to pull back. "Wow."

"I told you, and it was more than apparent she didn't want to talk to me."

"But she was forthcoming when she was interviewed at home."

I chuckled. "Yeah, and now I'm understanding why. That interview was on her own turf, and the mayor wasn't brought up. The interview was about George. Then I called her at work with questions about the mayor, and it instantly put her on the defensive."

Renz jotted down notes. "That's interesting."

"Damn straight it is, and she hasn't heard the last from me." I read through my notes. "So there's George's parents and Sheila Kam's son to interview in the next twenty-four hours, and we still haven't found any salacious news articles from the fifth of May that involved the mayor."

"Nope, we sure haven't."

I stood and headed for the door. "Come on. We need to have Taft set some priorities for the day. There's also the mayor's uncle and cousin who contested the latest family will. That had to cause bad blood."

"Right, and we need that warrant for the mayor's attorney's records. How much do you want to bet that the mayor's personal assistant and personal attorney know each other?"

"That's a sucker bet if I ever heard one. Of course they know each other, and we're going to find out why."

Chapter 38

I leaned against the wall in Maureen's office. I was too amped up to sit. We needed answers, and we needed them days ago. Killers were roaming the streets, one whose identity we knew for sure, yet they all remained invisible. We had to change that, and hopefully, once the TV news networks began airing their faces, we would get callers telling us where they might be hiding out.

Maureen began by asking what we'd found out in the last hour. Renz took the lead.

"We know that Julie Beckett and Douglas Blake aren't very cooperative, and it makes me wonder why."

Taft cocked her head. "Possibly hiding something?"

I laughed. "I'd say it's more probable than possible. It seems like their personalities change dramatically when questions are aimed directly at them."

"Sure, so what do you need from me?"

Renz said he would need a warrant for all billing, service, and phone records between Douglas Blake and Michael Kent going back at least a year.

"Done. What else?"

I wondered whether cleaning up messes was documented and what kind of records the mayor and Julie Beckett had kept. There had to be work-related documents concerning hours billed so the mayor would know how much the city had to pay her unless she was on retainer. Maureen said she'd get the judge to sign off on that too.

"You know if word gets out that warrants are being issued that involve Milwaukee's mayor, all hell is going to break loose with the press."

I shrugged. "It won't be a problem if nothing illegal comes to light. We're just doing our job by trying to find the maniacs who slaughtered ten innocent people, and as it stands, the people we've interviewed are the connections between the mayor and the victims, and now some of them don't want to talk."

That epiphany struck me like a lightning bolt. It was something that we'd discussed earlier. The only people who had a problem talking to us were the attorney, the personal assistant, and the mayor and his wife. The bartender and the owners of Silver Shores didn't take issue with us because they weren't personally acquainted with Michael Kent. That gave us even more reason to be suspicious and to expedite the warrants.

Maureen glanced at the clock. "I'll get the judge to move on those warrants as fast as humanly possible. The TV stations will start airing the breaking news about Cole, Lucas, and Erik at the top of the hour, so that means I'll have to alert the crew upstairs to be ready on the tip-line phones. Right now, we're in a holding pattern while we wait for those warrants, and to be honest, I don't think speaking to extended family will result in anything that'll help the case." Taft picked up the phone's receiver. "We need one more warrant, and it probably won't sit well with the judge."

I gave Renz a side-eyed glance. "And who is that warrant for?"

"If we're going to solve this case before more people die, we need to go to the source himself—the nexus. The warrant will be for the mayor, and all of you will go through his personal and work-related documents, as well as those of his attorney and his assistant, for the entire month of May." She looked from Renz to me. "Has anyone found anything incriminating that involved the mayor on the fifth of May?"

"Not to my knowledge, ma'am," I said.

Taft rubbed her chin. "That was an evening event with a speech from the mayor about the new firehouse, then dinner, and lastly the silent auction, correct?"

"That's what Amanda's parents said. An hour before and two hours after the fundraiser, people congregated at the bar to be entertained by Paul Lawrence."

"Hmm... so maybe there wouldn't be any news on that particular date. That could be why nobody has found anything involving the mayor on the fifth of May. Start looking at the headlines for the next day or even two days later."

"On it." Renz and I rushed to our office and began searching through the local news archives for all of May.

During the hour I searched, I couldn't find anything damning about the mayor. I slapped the desk in frustration with my open hand. "Seriously, Renz, what are we missing?"

He rolled his neck until it cracked. "I don't know, but whatever it is, it's buried big-time. My gut says the assistant and the attorney are knee-deep in a cover-up with the mayor. They wouldn't be squeamish about talking to us otherwise."

I agreed then propped my chin on my open hand and continued scrolling. "Wow, what a sad headline."

Renz gave me his full attention. "Yeah, what's that?"

"I didn't read the article, but it's something about five siblings who drowned when their van went into a lake just south of Capitol Drive. Sounds like they had been missing for a few days before the van was discovered."

Renz frowned. "They drown and the parents survived?"

"No, the vehicle was driven by the eldest sibling. I guess he was a nineteen-year-old man according to the article. The parents weren't with them."

"Yeah, sad stuff all right and probably a lot of guilt associated with it on the parents' part. Still nothing on the mayor?"

I shook my head. "I haven't found a damn thing. How about you?"

"Same."

Chapter 39

The group's morning meeting would be short and to the point. Everyone was skittish. The interruption last night by those FBI agents who were after Erik, Lucas, and Cole had made the entire group scatter before Jacob and Evelyn were able to share their updates.

Once again at the original gathering place in the abandoned warehouse, the meeting would reveal the people who would die next and the people who would be chosen as helpers. They would go to the final killings with Jacob and Evelyn and assist if necessary. After that, the group would disperse, go their own ways, and probably never see each other again unless a dramatic turn of events occurred.

Before the reveal, Jacob and Evelyn wanted details of how the agents were able to follow the guys to last night's location. Jacob jabbed the air as he pointed at Cole and demanded an explanation.

"I want to know how and why you led the FBI right to our doorstep."

Cole stammered as he tried to deflect the blame. It had been a clever setup by the police and FBI agents, and he would use that excuse to the best of his ability. "The cops came looking for Erik again. It was the third time that day that either they or the FBI showed up and pounded on the door. The FBI ransacked the apartment and took a jacket that belonged to Erik."

Jacob shot a glare Erik's way. "You and I will discuss that later." He jerked his head back at Cole. "Continue."

"The cops showed up again last night looking for Erik. It was time to leave for Barclay Street since you said to be there by ten. We watched out the window until the cops drove away, then we headed for the bus stop. Before we left the apartment, we looked up and down the street and didn't see anything that resembled a squad car or a cruiser, so we left. We had no idea that the bitch FBI agent who had harassed us earlier was waiting down the street. It's the only way she was able to follow the bus and us without our knowledge once we got off. When we saw headlights following us as we walked to the meeting place, I knew we'd been compromised. We lost them temporarily. I backtracked when I heard her talking on the phone and then clocked her in the face and took off. That's when we alerted everyone that she and the cops were on our trail. There's no way any of us can go back to the apartment now."

Erik took his turn. "Meaning we'll need a place to stay."

"Cole and Lucas can stay with Micah, and Erik, you can stay with us."

Evelyn began to protest. "But—"

Jacob put his finger to his lips. "Shh… I have a plan,

dear. I always do. Our original plan will have to wait for another day. Right now, I need to find out what I can about the FBI agent. You must have learned her name when she came looking for Erik, right, Lucas?"

"The other agent called her Jade. There can't be many local female agents with that name."

"And his name?"

"She called him Renz."

"Okay, everyone go home. Erik, you stick with us. I'll arrange another meeting for Thursday and let everyone know where it'll take place. Meanwhile, lay low and stay out of sight." Jacob jerked his head toward the broken-down doorway. "Now go and remain indoors. I'll let you know when it's safe to come out."

When the rest of the group was out of earshot, Jacob turned to Erik. "Why did the FBI take your jacket?"

He stared at the floor for a good twenty seconds before responding. "They must have figured out I was wearing it when I shot Brandon."

Jacob cocked his head. "And how would they know that?"

Erik shrugged dismissively, and in a flash, Jacob slapped his face.

"I see you aren't taking this mission as seriously as I thought you were. Nobody crosses me or takes needless risks without paying the piper."

Erik rubbed his reddened cheek. "What is that supposed to mean?"

"It means they've likely had that jacket tested for GSR,

211

and there's probably a warrant out for your arrest. Somehow, they found you on video Sunday morning. I told you to shoot him where there wasn't any cameras nearby."

"I swear, I didn't see cameras anywhere."

Evelyn huffed. "Obviously, they were there. You just didn't look hard enough."

Jacob continued where Evelyn left off. "Now, because of your carelessness, you'll end up being the decoy. You're going to lead them to a location I choose where we'll be waiting on the sidelines. From that point on, we'll follow that Jade woman wherever she goes until she goes home, unless I can find out where she lives through an internet search. I'm going to have someone that neither of you know shadow you, so if you don't do exactly as I say, I'll have that person take you out. Do you understand me because we didn't come this far to have everything go to shit."

"Yes, I understand."

"Good. Now, let's go back to our house so I can find out the full name of that FBI agent Jade, what she drives, where she lives, who if anyone she lives with, when she works, and how we're going to draw her in."

Chapter 40

We gathered in the lunchroom since the local TV stations were about to air the breaking news on Erik, Cole, and Lucas. We had two minutes before the news would begin, and the last commercial had just started. I had enough time to grab a coffee and sit down.

The main focus—and the most detailed information—would be on Erik since the GSR on his jacket had led us to believe he was Brandon's murderer. Both videos were shown on the news, including the one of him following Brandon and us on Hemmer Street and the one of him walking out of the alley after leaving Brandon dead in the stolen car. His police mug shot and those of Cole Pratt and Lucas Freeman were also aired along with the physical descriptions and information on the crimes committed by each man. Plastering their images on every news channel across Milwaukee and the surrounding counties was all we could do for the time being. Our agents answering the tip-line calls would take the information and pass it on to us, and we'd follow up on each tip that seemed legitimate. We planned to enlist the help of the local police departments, too, whenever necessary.

After watching the coverage on several stations, we headed to our offices and continued searching the archived files as we waited for the warrants to come in.

I had already searched through the eighth of May without a single negative article on the mayor. There were plenty of front- and second-page stories involving his activities throughout Milwaukee, the bills he'd signed into law, and the ceremonial events he'd attended. He had more or less the same routine every day.

Renz's phone rang, and he spoke for only a second before hanging up.

"It's go time. Taft has the warrants, and she said to come to her office immediately."

We reached her office at the same time the rest of our team did. She pointed to groups of two as she passed out the warrants. "Jade and Lorenzo, you go to the mayor's home. Tommy and Fay, you're in charge of the personal assistant's office and home. Mike and Carl, you're taking the attorney's office and home, and Charlotte and Kyle, you're working with the tip calls and will follow up on the most promising sightings first. If too many legit-sounding calls come in, I'll ask for help from that neighborhood's local precinct. Go on and head upstairs now. Tommy, Fay, Mike, and Carl, hit the attorney's office and the mayor's personal assistant's office first since it's a workday. They should be there. Their homes can be searched later, but don't let either of them make any calls in case somebody is at their house who can destroy evidence. The warrants for their phone records should be here this afternoon, and we can check those online when they arrive."

Tommy jerked his head toward the door. "Okay, we're on it."

The four agents walked out with the warrants, leaving Renz and me alone with Taft.

"How are we supposed to handle this with the mayor, Maureen?" Renz asked. "You know we're going to get plenty of blowback."

"Too bad. This is a murder investigation, and we have a job to do. Nobody is above the law, not even the mayor or his minions. If he's the reason people are being killed, then I want to know why. I don't care if he or his wife protest, I want you both to search their home from top to bottom. Tomorrow, you can go through his office at city hall. There's no excuse they can give or any person they can call that can legally block a search warrant, so they'll either need to leave the premises or stay put and deal with it. I'd suggest the latter since if they did leave, the mayor might go to his office and try to destroy evidence that might be there. If they do leave, they'll have the PD waiting at city hall for them. You can also remind the mayor that going to city hall would make the media curious."

"Got it." I pocketed the warrant, sucked in a deep breath—since I knew full well that the Kent's would resist our entry to the home—and we left. Once in the car, I turned to Renz as I buckled my seat belt. "So how bad do you think this is going to be?"

"Pretty bad. Put on your big-girl pants because I'm sure they'll try to keep us out the second they hear who we are through the gate intercom."

I shook my head as Renz merged onto the freeway and aimed the cruiser north. "Damn it, I sure love my job."

We reached the Kent compound twenty minutes later, and Renz pulled alongside the call box at the walled entrance. He pressed the button on the intercom and waited. It took a minute, but a female voice finally answered. I recognized it as Marie Kent's.

"Kent residence, how can I help you?"

Renz leaned out the car window and spoke into the call-box microphone. "Mrs. Kent, it's Agents DeLeon and Monroe. We have a search warrant for your residence. You need to buzz us through the gate."

"I will do no such thing. How dare you come to our private home in our time of grieving. We demand privacy! Leave us alone, or I'll call the police."

"Sorry, ma'am, but it doesn't work that way. This warrant gives us the legal right to enter your residence. If you resist, I'll be forced to call the police and have them escort us in. I doubt if you want your gate broken or the publicity that can draw. Do you want the media camped out on your lawn?"

"Of course not. You may not realize this, Agent DeLeon, but we're a prominent family in the city and don't take frivolous accusations lightly. Our lawyer will definitely be in touch with your superior. What grounds do you have to barge in on us like this?"

"Ma'am, nobody has accused you of anything yet, and your lawyer is also being served a warrant as we speak. For now, I'd suggest you calm down and let us do our job. Everything you need to know is stated in the warrant, which I'll gladly hand over to you once we enter. It's your choice—deal with us or deal with the police and the media."

The call box went silent, and the gate creaked open. Renz drove through and parked next to the brick sidewalk that led to the front door. I grabbed the warrant, and we exited the cruiser.

Marie Kent was already at the door, one hand on her hip and the other outstretched and waiting to snatch the warrant away from me.

"You'll be sorry you did this." She spewed threats at us with her eyes darting back and forth between Renz and me.

"Ma'am, I wouldn't advise threatening the FBI. It won't sit well if we do find anything incriminating. Where's your husband?" I asked.

She tipped her head reluctantly toward the library. "He's in there, and just so you know, he isn't sober."

I spoke up. "That seems to be an ongoing problem with the mayor, Mrs. Kent. How do you keep that from leaking out to the press?"

She huffed. "I'm not telling you anything."

I nodded. "Okay, then I'd suggest you take a seat and read through the warrant."

The home was massive, and just by the number of rooms on the first floor, I knew it would take all day to go through every nook, cranny, closet, and drawer in the entire house. We weren't even sure what we were looking for. I imagined finding a slip of paper, perhaps a confession to a wrongdoing that might have pissed someone off enough to commit the horrific murders. I knew we wouldn't find that, and I was doubtful that we would discover any confession at all. Logic told me that if there were clues that we could track, they would be in the form of bank statements that showed recurring payments to someone, email confessions, repeated calls to the same number, or text messages. A bit overwhelmed about where to start, I approached Renz.

"What should we do first? This home is enormous."

"First, we need to speak with the mayor if he's capable of putting a sentence together. He has to be told that we're here and why."

I rolled my eyes. "Do *we* even know why we're here beyond a theory?"

"No, but they don't need to know that. Let's check on his condition and then begin. If there's anything that could incriminate him, it'll likely be in the desk in the library, on his computer, or in his bedroom suite in a drawer." Renz headed for the library. "And we may have to take that computer back with us to Tech if it's password protected."

I had to agree and then mentioned my thoughts about the bank statements, text messages, and phone calls.

"We'll go through everything in the house, and if those types of items aren't here or at his office, we'll subpoena the bank statements too. If he's done anything wrong at all, there's a trail that leads back to him somewhere."

I rubbed my chin as I thought. "And I bet that trail is directly linked to his attorney or the personal assistant."

We entered the library to find the mayor slumped in his

wingback chair and facing the expansive window that overlooked the lake. He wasn't staring out, though—he was passed out, and the bottle of bourbon in his hand was teetering and ready to fall to the floor. I removed it, placed it on the desk, and called his name. He grumbled and began to snore.

"Wow, he's lived a privileged life forever, but his entire existence is reduced to a bottle of booze." I frowned at Renz. "Why wouldn't he get help?"

"Don't know, Jade, but that's on the mayor and his wife. If he can fake his way through his obligation to the citizens of Milwaukee, that's his cross to bear, and I'm sure his entire staff covers for him."

I looked around at the ornate wall coverings and imported furniture. I stared out the window across the lush gardens and at the beautiful blue lake. I sighed. "His life is nothing more than a sad façade. What a waste."

Renz walked to the desk and pulled open the top drawer. We searched for something that could tell us why ten people had been needlessly murdered.

We spent the next four hours going through the house from top to bottom with our focus on finding documents that showed a payout to *someone* to keep quiet about *something*. We came up empty. We found Marie in the living room, reading a book. She looked up and glared.

"Are you done yet?"

"We are for now." I took a seat across from her on a blue velvet chair. "Why don't you just tell us how the mayor is involved in the killings? The people who had a loved one murdered are all in one way or another linked to the mayor."

She shook her head. "Theories, nothing but theories. It's all you have, and if you don't mind, I'd like to be left alone now."

I sighed and stood. "Come on. Let's go."

Renz turned back and addressed Marie. "We can come back at any time, and Michael's office is next. People are going to start talking when they see the FBI in city hall, tearing apart the mayor's office." Renz waited as if he expected her to confess, but she remained tight-lipped. "Have it your way. We'll see ourselves out, and I'm taking the computer and his cell phone with me. I left documents on the desk that stated what was removed from the premises."

Renz and I walked out. It was late afternoon, and city hall would close in fifteen minutes.

I climbed in the passenger side and buckled up after Renz put the bagged computer and cell phone on the back seat. "I'll call Taft and see what she wants us to do."

Renz drove down the driveway and rattled his fingertips on the steering wheel as he waited for the gate to open. "I swear I'm stumped."

I looked his way. "So am I, partner. So am I."

Chapter 41

The other cruisers were in their designated parking spaces when we returned to our headquarters. By all appearances, everyone was back. I was excited to learn whether anything was found at the attorney and personal assistant's offices. Their homes would be searched later, possibly by our evening crew unless our team had already found evidence. I took the elevator with Renz. I didn't have time to run up three flights of stairs, and when we reached our floor, we went directly to Taft's office.

I knocked on her half-open door, and Maureen waved us in. She tipped her wrist and checked the time since we had been gone for hours. "Anything?"

The bagged computer and phone were still under Renz's arm. "Nothing that slapped us across the face as a confession, but I took the computer and the mayor's cell phone anyway. Tech can see what's on them as soon as the phone warrant comes in."

"Go ahead and drop those items off with Tech. The phone warrants should arrive anytime now."

"Good."

Taft continued. "So how did the mayor take your intrusion?"

I rolled my eyes. "He didn't even know we were there. The man was passed out drunk."

"Hmm… that makes me wonder."

Renz raised a brow. "Wonder what?"

"If he's that way all the time or only because of Tamara's murder."

I shrugged. "Who knows, but Marie Kent doesn't seem at all surprised or angered by it. It's like she's used to seeing her husband that way."

"And maybe the mayor's staff is, too, unless he can get by during work hours without a drink," Renz said.

Maureen waved us on. "Gather the rest of the group and drop off that computer and phone. We'll meet in the conference room in five minutes now that everyone is back."

Minutes later, as we sat at our regular seats, we waited for Charlotte and Kyle to join us. According to Taft, they had followed up on two tip-line sightings of Erik and Cole, but neither had panned out. They were back upstairs and about to come down to join the meeting.

As soon as they entered, Taft began. She addressed her first questions to Tommy and Fay. "What did you find in Julie Beckett's office?"

"Not a damn thing except a furious personal assistant whose face had gone beet red. I'm sure if there was some communication between her and the mayor on the night of May fifth, it was via email, text, or phone calls. There's no reason to have incriminating paper documents lying around unless somebody had to sign something. I think searching the phone records is the way to go."

Renz cut in. "We have the mayor's cell phone and computer. Once Tech gains access to them, we'll likely learn a lot."

Carl and Mike's account of the search at the attorney's office proved to have the same result—nothing there that incriminated him.

"Okay, if either of them had contact with the mayor on the night of May fifth, it'll show up in all three phone records. There could be texts still on the mayor's phone, or he could have deleted them, but the records would reflect that."

I tipped my head at Charlotte. "So two false sightings?"

"Not sure if either was false. It's just that nobody who fits the description of Erik or Cole was in the area when law enforcement got there seconds after the calls. When we arrived, we scoured the neighborhoods ourselves and found nothing. Chasing calls when the alleged suspect is on the move is useless. We can't track them that way. Somebody has to see them enter stores or houses or know where they're hiding out."

Taft turned to Renz. "How soon before Tech can get into the phone?"

"They said within the hour."

"And Mrs. Kent wouldn't tell you anything?"

"Not a damn word."

"What about the archived news articles involving the mayor?"

"Nothing beyond the typical duties he performs every day," I said.

"Okay, for now, everyone head upstairs and lend a hand going through the tip-line calls. Something we can track has to come through sooner or later—and preferably sooner."

Chapter 42

"Tell us everything you can remember about that female FBI agent," Jacob said. He, Evelyn, and Erik sat around the kitchen table with the laptop opened to the local FBI's website. "I have to find out her last name and where she lives. After that, we need to know if there's someone in her life that she cares deeply about. I want her to feel the same anguish as the families who played a part in destroying our lives. The people who own Silver Shores, the bartender who thinks his carnival tricks are entertaining, the attorney and assistant who covered up the mayor's sins, and the mayor himself." Jacob glanced at the wall clock. "Someone will die tonight, but it won't be the mayor. He's being saved for last—the grand finale—and maybe even with that FBI agent at his side. One thing I know for sure is, if she gets in the way of our plans, she won't live to see another day."

Erik described in detail what Jade looked like—shoulder-length black hair, jade-green eyes, tall and slender, and probably in her late thirties. Jacob scrolled through the FBI's website, but none of the agents' names, biographies, or photos were shown.

"Damn it. Guess using an abundance of caution is the FBI's motto. There's nothing about any agent at all."

Jacob continued looking online for several hours, going through archived FBI takedowns and noting which agents were involved, their merit awards, promotions, and so on until he found it. An article from nearly four years prior showed a local news photograph from a graduation ceremony for newly minted FBI agents. Jade stood in the second row, and because of her height, she was easy to see. Jacob tapped her name on the computer screen and fist-pumped the air.

"I finally found her. The bitch's name is Jade Monroe. Now I can do an online search to learn more about her and where she lives."

Jacob's mind flashed back to Erik's carelessness. Because of that, the FBI knew his name, where he had lived, and with whom. They also were aware of his arrest record and the crimes he'd committed in the past that could link him to vigilante or extremist groups in the area.

He isn't worth hanging on to, and as long as Cole and Lucas stay under the radar, they'll live to see another day. It's time to cut off our affiliation with Erik—literally.

Jacob rose from his chair and temporarily powered down the computer. He needed to have a private conversation with Evelyn about Erik's fate and who would be enlisted to do the deed. It had to be someone whom Erik didn't know, and it had to take place before dark. Jacob had heard on the scanner earlier that Erik, Cole, and Lucas had APBs out on them. Jacob had already told Erik he was going to be a decoy as a punishment, but Erik had no idea that the plan was about to change.

Jacob led Evelyn into their bedroom and closed the door at his back.

She took a seat on the blanket chest and faced her husband. "What's wrong?"

"Nothing, but Erik needs to be eliminated. Brandon was a risk we couldn't afford, and now Erik is too. We have to complete what we started. It's God's will."

Evelyn nodded. "What do you suggest?"

"Erik knows he has to perform a duty for us as a way to repent of his careless behavior. I'm going to send him to the bus stop on Downer and Newport. He'll sit in the shelter and wait for my call. I'll tell him that call is his signal to run because the cops are on their way. Meanwhile, I'll have someone he doesn't know take a seat next to him as if he's also waiting for the bus. What Erik doesn't know is that person is going to knife him in the lungs, kill him, and go about his day. He won't know that the police were never coming, but once I hear on the scanner that somebody actually found Erik dead in the bus shelter and the cops are en route, we'll take our position to watch the drama unfold. They'll know who Erik is within minutes, alert the FBI, and that's when the fun will begin. We'll follow Agent Monroe everywhere she goes until she calls it a night at her own home. We'll find out even more about her after that. When I told Erik that somebody was going to die that night, he probably didn't realize I meant it would be him."

Evelyn nodded. "So who's going to do the deed?"

"I'll call James. He owes me a favor, and Erik doesn't know him."

"Good choice. He'll get it done, and we'll move forward with our plans. We're getting close to the end, Jacob, and we'll finally right the wrong that has been covered up for nearly five and a half months. The city is about to learn the truth, and we'll have the satisfaction of exacting our revenge on all who were involved. The Bible says an eye for an eye and a tooth for a tooth, and no matter what, we're not about to turn the other cheek."

Jacob grasped the doorknob. "So we're in agreement? I should call James?"

"Yes, do it now. The sooner we accomplish our mission the sooner we'll have closure."

They walked out of the bedroom and saw Erik sitting in the living room, staring at his phone. Jacob asked for his attention. "We've come up with a plan. I want you to go to the bus stop at Downer and Newport. You'll sit there and do nothing until I call you. When I do, you'll take off, get lost in the neighborhood, then return to the house. Meanwhile, we'll be there watching once the cops arrive."

"How will the cops know I'm there?"

"There's an APB out for you, Cole, and Lucas, but you're the main person they're looking for because of Brandon."

Erik stared at the floor and kept silent.

"I'll call in the sighting, then I'll be listening to the scanner. When the cops are within a block of you, I'll call your phone. That'll be your cue to get the hell out of there.

Evelyn and I will already be somewhere nearby so we can watch the scene play out, and hopefully, Agent Monroe will show up. I'm assuming when they realize nobody fitting your description is there, they'll leave, and maybe she'll just head home. No matter what, we'll follow her. We're trying to draw her in and then take her out so she doesn't interfere with our mission. We intend to complete the entire plan by Thursday night, and I don't want any hiccups from the FBI. Do you understand your instructions?"

"Yes. Sit in the bus shelter until you call me and then run back to the house before the cops arrive."

"Exactly, and speak to nobody." Jacob checked the time. "Go ahead. We want it to still be light outside when they arrive in case the agent is with them. I want a positive ID of her, and then we'll take it from there. The walk is only five blocks. Keep your head down until you get there, and then run like hell when I call you. The key to the back door is on top of the coach light."

Erik stood and walked to the door. "I promise I won't let you down."

Jacob smiled. "Good, because I'm counting on you."

Chapter 43

Wearing one of Jacob's sweatshirts, Erik kept his head down as he took the fifteen-minute walk to the bus shelter. He knew Jacob was disappointed in his mistakes. After shooting Brandon, Erik had left at the apartment the jacket that he'd worn while committing the murder. Checking for gunshot residue had to be the only reason the FBI showed up for the second time, took the jacket, and left. The only way they would have made the connection with the jacket was if there actually was a camera in that alley area and Erik had overlooked it. He must have walked into the frame, and the FBI recognized him and his jacket and came calling. The county crime lab had to have found GSR on the sleeves, or Erik wouldn't be wanted for murder.

He couldn't believe how badly he'd messed up. Now he had to pay the price and complete his task, and hopefully, he would be forgiven. He had to do better going forward.

Erik reached the bus shelter and took a seat. He stared at the intersection and watched traffic go by as he waited for the call from Jacob. A man wearing a gray hoodie gave him a nod as he took a seat to Erik's left. Neither man spoke.

Erik had been told to keep quiet, sit patiently, and leave immediately when the call came in.

Several minutes passed in silence, then Erik grunted loudly and doubled over. He gasped for air as a sharp pain overtook his left side.

The stranger next to him pushed the knife deeply into Erik's left lung and twisted the handle. The man pulled out the knife and buried it once more, that time in Erik's left kidney, until Erik collapsed against the side of the shelter. The man took Erik's phone from his pocket and walked away.

The last words Erik heard were "The deed is done."

Chapter 44

We'd been upstairs, separating the realistic leads from the absurd ones, when Renz's cell phone rang. He pulled it from his pocket, spoke for a second, then rushed all of us downstairs to Taft's office once more.

Maureen didn't have time to elaborate about the phone call she'd just received, but in a few sentences, she'd said we needed to get to the intersection of Downer and Newport immediately. A man had just arrived at the bus shelter there and originally thought the man next to him was a sleeping homeless person until he saw the blood on the seat. He called the nearest police station, and two units arrived and realized the dead man was none other than Erik Smalley, the alleged murderer who had an APB and warrant out for his arrest.

We headed out in two cruisers with lights flashing and made it to the scene in twenty minutes. The police had already cordoned off the entire block around the bus shelter and had diverted traffic to parallel streets.

There was only an hour left before night would take over the sky, and we needed to see what we could while we still had daylight. We pulled out our IDs as the team dipped under the police tape and headed straight for the body. From fifty feet away, I could already see that the dead man was Erik. He was slumped against the right Plexiglas wall of the shelter. Blood had pooled on the seat next to him and dripped to the concrete floor after drenching his sweatshirt.

The forensic team arrived just after us and took over the scene. I was thankful they would be able to get decent pictures before it was too dark. We backed away temporarily and asked the officers for details of the moments they got there and who the caller was. Charlotte and Kyle spoke to them at the barricade while Renz and I followed up with the 911 caller as he sat in the back of a squad car. We needed his account of everything he'd seen and done before realizing the man in the shelter was dead. The rest of our team canvassed the area and spoke with the onlookers. According to everyone's account, they hadn't seen anything out of the ordinary, and that response seemed to come more frequently every time we asked. People seemed to live in a cell phone bubble and didn't pay much attention to anything beyond that three-by-five-inch screen in front of their noses. The only person with anything to say was the caller, and we listened carefully to his every word.

When I heard doors open and close, I glanced back at the scene. The county ME, Dave Mann, had arrived. There wasn't too much of a guess about Erik's time of death, which had happened within the last half hour or so, but there was a chance that before he took the body back to the autopsy room, Dave could tell us something about the weapon used. I returned my focus to the 911 caller, Don Reddig, who said he took the early-evening bus to work every night. That time was no different than any other until he saw the blood pool next to the man he thought was sleeping. He said he called 911 immediately and backed out of the shelter.

"Did you see anyone milling around the shelter as if they were there to watch what was unfolding?" Renz asked.

Don shook his head. "I was so alarmed, I didn't even notice. I was just hoping the police would arrive before anyone else stepped into the shelter."

"Did anybody walk out of the shelter when you approached it?" I asked.

"No, and I only passed one person who was walking toward me on the sidewalk."

"Can you describe that person?"

Don frowned at Renz. "Sorry, but no. He was wearing a gray hoodie. That's all I remember."

"Okay, that helps." I glanced at both sides of the street and saw plenty of opportunity for cameras that might face the bus shelter. I excused myself and went to talk to the rest of our team and the officers who were already there. As far as I was concerned, the local precinct should have their detectives follow up on camera footage. We needed to focus entirely on finding out who'd killed Erik and the others. In my opinion, the people calling the shots were eliminating their own to keep them from talking if they were ever apprehended. That meant Cole and Lucas, wherever they were, were likely in imminent danger too.

I called Taft, updated her on what we had, and gave her my suggestion about having local detectives work the camera end of the investigation. I told her that a man wearing a gray hoodie had walked toward Don Reddig as he approached the shelter and could be a person of interest. She said she would call the district's police chief and give him our recommendations.

After hanging up, I headed toward Dave. Renz met me at the shelter and said he'd given Don his card in case he remembered anything more.

I pointed my chin at the ME. "Know anything, Dave? Is it a gunshot?"

"Nope. No stippling or gunshot burns on the clothing, and from how the wounds are shaped, I'd go with a large knife as the weapon."

"Wounds? There was more than one?"

"I've found two entry spots where the blood is heaviest on the sweatshirt. One between the ribs and into his left lung, likely to disable him quickly, and the other right into his left kidney."

"So the killer sat on his left side as if he were another rider waiting for the bus?" Renz asked.

"That's the way I see it."

"Okay, good. If that man in the gray hoodie was actually in the shelter and sitting on Erik's left side, and nobody else entered or exited, then we know he's the killer. There's a chance that the cameras along Downer might be able to follow him to a house or a car," I said.

"What are we going to do about that?" Renz asked.

"Maureen is taking care of it since we already have our hands full with this investigation." I turned to Dave. "We're going to need his cell phone."

"There isn't one, only his wallet and some change."

"Damn it. Then we need to bag whatever is in his pockets and take it back with us."

Dave took care of that and handed the bag to me.

"Thanks." I pulled Renz aside. "Have you noticed anyone in the area showing too much interest?"

He shook his head. "I've already thought about that and told the rest of the gang to watch the crowd. So far, the onlookers seem like typical gawkers."

"Okay. I think a few of us should head back. Maureen said the phone warrants are in. We need to start comparing them to each other. It's the only way to get leverage. If we find something incriminating from the fifth of May or first thing the morning of the sixth that's between the attorney, the assistant, and the mayor, well, that's real evidence that they're hiding something. First one to cough up the truth gets the best deal. Ten lives were lost because of whatever that truth is."

Renz rounded up our team and told Tommy and Fay to come with us. The rest stayed at the scene to help out as necessary. Taft would call Kyle as soon as she wanted them back.

Chapter 45

"Looks like Agent Monroe and a few others are leaving." Jacob stared out the windshield with interest.

He and Evelyn sat in the car across the street in a food market parking lot and watched the commotion unfold. The police buzzed around like a swarm of bees, and when the FBI showed up and took over the scene, the police surrendered their command and adopted the role of lowly minions.

Evelyn huffed. "The typical chain of command like in all things. It's time for the little guy to stand up for what's right, and that's exactly what we're doing."

"Amen to that, honey. We probably have a long night ahead of us since Agent Monroe is getting into that cruiser with the other three. She doesn't appear to be going home yet. We're going to need someone else to watch her until she leaves for the night and then follow her home. I'll call Micah as soon as they arrive at wherever they're going. He can take over after that. We have too much to do tonight, and it's imperative we get it done without interruptions. Payback will begin tonight to those who deserve it."

Jacob pulled out of the lot and followed several car lengths behind the cruiser as it headed south. Once they reached the southern suburbs of Milwaukee, he was pretty certain of the agents' final destination. He'd done his research. They were going back to the FBI headquarters in St. Francis, and he would tell Micah to meet them across the street from the entrance to the compound. Jacob would forward Jade's photograph to Micah's cell phone so he'd know exactly who to follow. After that, they'd part ways, and he, Evelyn, Cole, and Lucas would meet on the block where the attorney lived. That night, two more people would be checked off their kill list.

Chapter 46

We were back at our headquarters by seven o'clock. With our supper of vending machine sandwiches in front of us, we sat at the conference room table with the printed-out phone records belonging to Michael Kent, Julie Beckett, and Douglas Blake. We were about to compare all the records from the beginning of May until the present. With records for the mayor, attorney, and assistant spread out before us, we looked for any matching phone numbers and connections. We'd circle every number that showed up on the records as matching the written ones. We needed to make a connection between the three on the same dates and relatively close to the same times. That would give us the connection, but to what, we still didn't know. By playing one person against the other, though, we were sure somebody would talk.

It didn't take long to find that a flurry of calls to each other had come in after eleven p.m. on May fifth. The above-average number of calls lasted through the next few days then tapered off to a typical level between the mayor and Julie Beckett and less frequently between the mayor and the attorney.

I leaned back and stared at the ceiling. "It's obvious that

the attorney and the assistant made something disappear that the mayor didn't want to go public. After the second week of May until now, there aren't any calls between the two. Douglas Blake and Julie Beckett worked hand in hand during that time but not again since."

"Yeah, great. Now all we have to do is find out what they were covering up for the mayor," Tommy said.

"Whatever the mayor did was bad enough to cause someone to commit murder, including murdering the mayor's own daughter. Wouldn't you think he'd be forthright about knowledge of possible suspects?" I asked.

Renz rubbed his chin. "Not if it incriminated him. Think about it. The Kent's are one of the most well-known families in the entire state. Not only is there the family legacy to uphold, but they're wealthy, influential, and he's the city mayor for God's sake. So—"

"So not revealing the people who killed his daughter, his attorney's mother-in-law, and his personal assistant's dearest friend is worth keeping quiet over?" Fay shook her head. "What is this world coming to?"

I tapped the sheet of phone records in front of me. "I'm thinking it's about self-preservation. All three of them could end up in prison for whatever the crime was. Were there text messages, too, or just the phone records?"

"No text messages that we can find right now," Renz said. "They've all been deleted. It'll take time to pull them back. At least, that's what John in Tech told Maureen."

"Damn it. Okay, what's bad enough to murder for?" I asked.

Fay spoke up first. "Money, betrayal, and causing the death of a loved one."

I looked at Renz and Tommy. "You guys have anything to add to that?"

"Well, there's several kinds of betrayal, as in marriage betrayal and business betrayal," Renz said.

"True, but what Fay just said makes me curious."

"Which part?" Tommy asked.

"About causing the death of a loved one. The mayor has more money than God, and his extended family has already tried to extort money out of the will. That didn't go anywhere. Michael Kent doesn't have a business partner per se, and Marie wouldn't be a likely candidate for an extramarital affair. She's pushing sixty and not at all sexy if you ask me."

"So, the mayor goes to the fundraiser and, what, drinks too much?" Fay asked.

Tommy nodded. "Yeah, Paul said he had to cut him off before the end of the night."

"Right," Renz said. "So he leaves drunk late at night but only has a few miles between Silver Shores and his house. It would be easy enough to see if there were any accidents reported along that stretch of road that night."

"But we've checked the mayor's driving record, and nothing came up," Fay said. "He's never been arrested for anything."

Renz slapped the table so hard I felt the vibration. "That's it! That's the cover-up. He hit somebody with his car when he was drunk and caused either their death or irreversible injuries. The victim was either in a car, or they were a pedestrian who was hit by the mayor's vehicle. There's no other explanation." Renz jerked his chin toward me. "Pull up Michael Kent's DMV records and see what kind of vehicle he owns."

I did and saw that he owned two cars, a 2018 BMW 5-series sedan and a 2019 Volvo wagon. "I'd put my money on him being the driver of the BMW. The mayor has to look sharp in public. Marie looks more like a Volvo wagon driver."

"Either way, if he had a damaged car and needed to get it repaired under the radar, then he likely had Doug or Julie pay for it with their own credit card and then gave them cash. We need to check their bank records then pull up Carfax reports on both the BMW and the Volvo."

"On it," Tommy said. "I'll check the Carfax, and Fay, you pull up Julie and Doug's bank records and check for any payment going to an automobile repair shop."

I was excited and felt we were close to solving the mystery—at lease about the cover-up, but we still needed to find out who the person was that the mayor had wronged.

After paying to see the report, Tommy entered the BMW's VIN into the Carfax website. "I've got it! There was a front-end repair made on the sixth of May at the BMW dealership in Whitefish Bay. The report shows the car is owned by Marie Claremont Kent."

"Marie's maiden name probably throws people off, and they don't realize she's the mayor's wife," Fay said.

I added my opinion. "And I bet the vehicles are in her name because the mayor is a high-risk driver due to his drinking problem."

Renz high-fived us. "Okay, let's tie all of this together and see who paid the bill."

I offered to pull up the lawyer's bank records while Fay pulled up Julie's. "The payment might not show up until June's billing cycle, so check June too."

Fay nodded as we both tapped our laptop keyboards and pulled up the bank statements. I scrolled through Doug's payments made via check, credit card, and debit card through May—nothing to the BMW dealership.

Fay yelled out. "Here it is! Julie Beckett made a debit card transaction to the BMW dealership in Whitefish Bay on the sixth of May."

"Okay, just to cover our asses, make sure she doesn't own a BMW herself," Renz said.

I pulled up her DMV records and saw that she owned a two-year-old Lexus SUV. "Nope, no BMW listed for her."

Renz reached for the landline phone on the table. "Time to question the three of them again. Their choice—either the nearest police station or in their home, but somebody is going to tell us what we want to know tonight."

Chapter 47

"Are you in place?"

"Yes. We're in the bushes along his garage. How soon should we expect you?"

Jacob glanced at the map on his phone. "We're following him, and he's only two blocks from his house. We'll be there in a minute. As soon as he pulls into the garage, slip in and grab him out of the car. Don't let him yell or honk the horn, so move fast. Evelyn and I will take care of the rest."

"Got it. We won't let you down."

Jacob stopped and waited at the end of the block as Douglas Blake turned in to his driveway. Once the attorney's vehicle cleared the garage door, Jacob pulled ahead and parked two houses away. He and Evelyn exited the car, rushed to the garage, and ducked under the door. When they saw that Douglas was restrained by Cole and Lucas, Jacob nodded to Evelyn. She crossed the garage and pressed the button on the wall, lowering the overhead.

Jacob walked to the writhing man and asked if he knew who he was.

"Of course I don't know who you are, you psycho! What do you want from me? My money, my car? Take them both, just leave me alone."

Jacob punched Douglas in the gut, doubling the man over. He gasped for air.

"Your money and car mean nothing to us. The only thing I want from you is your life. I want to watch you die. You covered up the mayor's sins, and his life went on. You denied he did anything wrong on the night of May fifth. You helped hide all evidence of his crime, and he walked away scot-free. Five long months have passed, and my wife and I thought about how we would avenge the deaths you caused. The only way was to make you suffer the same pain we felt and end your life as well. It's God's plan. We've prayed over it for months, and righteousness will prevail."

"What the hell are you talking about, all this religious blabbering? I have money and expensive watches in the house. You can have it all. Just leave me alone."

"Material things mean nothing to us. You've already taken our most precious assets." Jacob closed in until he was only inches from the attorney. Evelyn joined Jacob and stood at his side. With a quick glance at Cole, Jacob nodded, and Cole pulled back Douglas's head. Jacob slid his knife out of its sheath, and it glistened from the garage's overhead light.

"No, no! You can't kill me. I'll give you anything you want."

"You've already taken everything we've ever wanted." With a swift swipe, Jacob slashed the attorney's neck wide open. He moved aside as the blood sprayed outward with every heartbeat Douglas had left. Within a minute, the man went limp, and Cole let him fall to the floor.

"God's will was done. Grab the garage remote from his car and let's go."

Evelyn pressed the wall button, they all ducked under the door, then Cole pressed the remote to lower it. He tossed the remote into the storm drain, then they climbed into Jacob's car and drove away.

"One down and one to go." Evelyn patted her husband's shoulder. "I can feel the cloud of darkness begin to lift."

Chapter 48

Renz tried the attorney's number for the third time and finally gave up. "Maybe he went out to dinner with friends or is meeting with a client and silenced his ringer."

"Then let's try Julie Beckett," Fay said. "They both share equal guilt."

Renz dialed her number, and it went directly to voicemail. "What the hell? It's a Tuesday night, and tomorrow is a workday."

"So what should we do?" I asked. "We have proof that they called each other and the mayor on consecutive days and nights, but that in itself isn't a crime. We can't go in with guns blazing and arrest them for—"

"Yeah, for what?" Tommy asked.

"That's the problem, but we can make innuendos. We don't know what the crime was yet, but they don't know that. Maybe we can scare them into talking," I said. "I for one would like to stop the murders as soon as possible."

Renz frowned. "You can't possibly want to sit on their doorstep until someone comes home. Maybe it would be better to wait until morning when we know they've gone to work. They can't hide from us there."

"I even called Rebecca Kam to ask where Doug is, but she's in Chicago until tomorrow so she doesn't know. She's there to deal with some of her mom's estate."

"In Chicago?" Renz asked.

"Properties Sheila Kam co-signed on years ago, I guess." I pointed my thumb over my shoulder. "I'll see what Taft wants us to do. I need some exercise anyway." I walked the hallway to Maureen's office and fired off a quick text to Amber saying I'd be home when I got home and not to wait up. At Maureen's door, I saw her packing it up for the night. It was almost eight o'clock. I gave her a quick update, telling her we'd discovered multiple calls between the three of them on the night of May fifth and then more during the next week but still didn't know what they were covering up.

"I was just coming down to speak with you guys. I think you'll need to talk with Mr. Blake and Ms. Beckett face-to-face."

"That's what Renz suggested, but neither answer their phones."

"Then we'll haul them in for questioning in the morning then go directly to the mayor's mansion and question him as well." Maureen tipped her wrist. "You four go home. I'm sure the rest of the team already did. Everything will come to light tomorrow after talking with them. They're in this together, and we'll play them against each other."

"You sure?"

"I'm sure. You've all been putting in twelve-hour days." Maureen turned off her office light and closed the door. She pointed her chin toward the end of the hall. "Tell everyone to shut it down. That's enough for tonight."

"Yes, ma'am."

I returned to the conference room and passed along Maureen's message. Tomorrow, we would surprise Douglas Blake and Julie Beckett at work, and if they weren't cooperative there, we'd escort them to the nearest police station for taped questioning. I looked forward to going home and plopping down in my bed. Although the case was local, it seemed even more draining than when we were on the road in other states. Because of the number of people killed and without knowing a solid motive for the crime, or even who'd committed the murders, I was exhausted.

If I was lucky, I would get eight glorious hours of uninterrupted sleep, and we'd call the case a wrap tomorrow then move on to the next one.

Chapter 49

Jacob wiped the blood from his hands onto Julie's pants. She was the second person to die that night, and his feeling of elation was well worth the wait. God would forgive him if he repented. He knew that to be true. Jacob was well-versed in the writings of the Bible.

The call he'd been anticipating was coming in from Micah, and that call would tie everything together and set the final play in motion. After speaking at length with Evelyn about the owners of Silver Shores and the bartender, Paul Lawrence, they'd decided not to kill them. They hadn't deliberately sided with the mayor and likely didn't even know about his crime. They'd only provided the venue and the booze that allowed the mayor to make his fatal error that night. Three people were responsible for that cover-up, and two were already dead. Jacob stared at Julie's body riddled with knife wounds, spat on her, then answered the call from Micah.

"Is she home?"

"Yes, she just pulled into her garage. There's two other cars there, one in the garage and one outside. I took pictures of both plate numbers."

"Good, so do your due diligence and find out who they are. I don't believe Agent Monroe is married, but find out for sure. I need to know who else lives in that house. Whoever it is that Jade Monroe loves the most will die tomorrow. She needs to feel the pain just like the others did. We could have completed this mission days ago if the FBI hadn't interfered, so call me as soon as you know who those vehicles belong to."

"I will, and tomorrow morning, I'll snatch one of them for you if you like."

"We'll do it together after I find out who they are, then we'll tie it in with the final plan."

Jacob ended the call and turned to his helpers, Cole and Lucas. They had completed their mission that night. Jacob and Evelyn thanked them for jobs well done, and they said their goodbyes. They might never meet again, and Jacob suggested the men move on to another city where they would be safer.

They parted ways with wishes of good luck, then Jacob and Evelyn drove home. Tomorrow would be the grand finale, but they needed one more person in their custody to make it all worthwhile.

The call came in more than an hour later. It was Micah again.

Jacob cleared his throat before answering. "What did you find out?"

"Good news. The car in the driveway belongs to the agent's sister, who happens to be a detective at the Washburn County Sheriff's Office."

Jacob laughed. "This is just getting better and better. And the other car?"

"Another detective from the sheriff's office but not related to the Monroe sisters."

"Then we need to focus on the sister. Given the fact that Agent Monroe has much farther to drive to work than the other two, I'd imagine she leaves first every morning. We'll be there waiting and might have to deal with the sister and the other woman if they drive to work together, but we'll cross that bridge when we get to it. Be at my house by six a.m. tomorrow. It looks like we'll be driving to North Bend early in the morning."

Chapter 50

"Why did you park outside, Amber? I thought it was Kate's week to drive." I bit off another piece of my cream-cheese-slathered bagel and washed it down with a gulp of coffee.

"Jack wants to go over my yearly review before everyone shows up, and Kate has a dentist appointment at one o'clock anyway."

"Got it, and good luck with the review." I grabbed my purse and briefcase and headed to the garage door. "Tell Jack it better be a good one, or I'll come after him."

Amber laughed. "I doubt if he's afraid of you. When it comes to one-on-one combat, he can easily take you, Sis. Sorry, but it's true."

I feigned hurt feelings then grinned. "Maybe so, but I have seniority over him. He can't change that." I waved goodbye, raised the overhead, and backed out of the garage with hopes that the Milwaukee traffic wouldn't be a nightmare that Wednesday morning.

Luckily, without a traffic bottleneck slowing me down on the freeway, I was at work by seven forty-five. We needed to organize our plan of how to approach Douglas Blake and

Julie Beckett, and both would have to be confronted at the same time. We couldn't risk either of them calling the other to give a warning that we were there.

Renz spoke up. "According to Douglas Blake's website, his office doesn't open until nine a.m. By the time we finalize our plan and get to city hall, it'll be close to nine o'clock."

Taft agreed. "Where exactly is Mr. Blake's office?"

"Somewhere downtown, so the police precinct will be the same for both city hall and the attorney's office."

Maureen continued. "Okay, split up and go to city hall and the attorney's office, take Mr. Blake and Ms. Beckett to the downtown precinct, and question them there. Make sure you arrive at the police station at the same time so they see each other. That in itself will cause one of them to start talking right away."

"Sounds like a plan," Tommy said. "After one of them starts singing like a canary and we find out how the mayor is involved, we'll hit his residence. He may very well be arrested today and taken into custody if it's warranted."

Maureen held Mike and Carl back. Once we knew what was going on, they would be dispatched to the mayor's residence and wait for the rest of us to arrive.

We left our headquarters at eight thirty and took two cruisers. It would be a fifteen-minute drive to downtown Milwaukee in the morning traffic, then we'd have to park wherever we could snag a spot and go through security at city hall. Renz, Tommy, and I were tasked to that building, while Fay, Kyle, and Charlotte took the attorney's office, which had a private parking lot.

Once we had passed through security and reached the administrative wing which housed the mayor's office, I called Tommy's phone and told him that they should enter the attorney's office—we were in place.

We were instantly stopped by the gatekeeper, but with badges in hand, we continued past her. We reached Julie Beckett's office, pushed open the door, and found it empty. We turned back.

Tommy took the lead at the gatekeeper's desk. "Where is Julie Beckett?"

"She isn't here," the woman hissed. "She never came to work today, and she didn't call in either, but you barged past me before I could tell you that."

I gave Renz a frown when I remembered that we couldn't reach her the night before either. Right then, Renz's cell phone rang. He talked for several seconds then hung up. He jerked his chin toward the outer hallway, and we followed him out.

"That was Kyle. He said the attorney hasn't shown up for work this morning and his staff can't reach him."

"What the hell is going on?" I asked. "We couldn't get ahold of him last night either."

"Okay, we need to go to their residences and see if they're home. There's the chance they're both on the run if they know we're close to finding out the real story of May fifth. Let's go."

I called Kyle as we walked to the parked cruiser. "Kyle, you guys need to go to Douglas Blake's house and see if he's there. He might be on the run. We're heading to Julie Beckett's house too. I imagine Renz told you she wasn't at work. Keep us posted."

I hung up and climbed into the back seat. Tommy peeled away from the curb just as I slammed the back door. We reached Julie's house twenty minutes later and headed up the sidewalk. Tommy gave the door several hard raps, and we waited longer than it should have taken for anyone to answer—unless they were avoiding the cops. I jerked my head at the guys.

"I need your help at the garage door." They followed me to the overhead, where I pointed at the small decorative windows at the top of the door. "Give me a boost and don't drop me." I stepped on Tommy's entwined fingers and grasped Renz's shoulder as they boosted me up long enough for me to see inside the garage. "Damn it, guys, her car is inside." I stepped down, and we returned to the front door and pounded again. Nobody answered. "What do you think? Should we kick in the door?"

Renz rounded the house with Tommy and me on his heels. He pushed up on every window that he passed. I'd hoped for a slider patio door but no luck. Julie had French doors with sheer drapes over them. We couldn't open the door or see inside unless we broke one of the window panels.

"One piece of glass is cheaper than breaking down a door," I said. "I think we need to do an emergency wellness check."

"I agree." With his jacket on to prevent glass cuts,

Tommy hit the pane of glass nearest the door lock with his elbow. The glass fell to the floor, and he reached in and unlocked the door. The thought of breaking into somebody's home that easily and quickly was unnerving, especially since it was obvious that Julie didn't have an alarm system.

We stepped over the glass and called out to her but didn't get a reply.

"Don't touch anything," Renz said. "This entire house could be a crime scene."

We called out again with guns drawn as we divided up and cleared each room. It didn't appear that there was a forced entry or an altercation until I reached the master bedroom.

"Oh my God! Guys, get in here." Renz and Tommy had been clearing the opposite end of the house.

Julie lay on the floor inside her bedroom, half in the walk-in closet and half out. She had been brutally murdered, possibly with a knife, and had what looked like stab wounds all over her body. From the position she lay in, it seemed that the perp could have been lying in wait in the closet and attacked her when she opened the door.

"Shit," Renz said as he and Tommy rounded the corner. "I better warn the others. There's a chance that Douglas Blake may have met the same fate."

Kyle answered Renz's call on the second ring. From the conversation we heard when Renz set his phone on Speaker, they were looking at the throat-slashed body of Douglas Blake lying on his garage floor.

"Damn it," Renz said. "Secure the scene. I need to call Taft and update her. Meanwhile, call the ME and Forensics, tell them we have two crime scenes, and ask if they can get extra manpower to pitch in. Stay put, and we will too. Taft needs to contact the police and have them secure the mayor's house. She'll likely send Mike and Carl there as well."

"I'll make the call now. We should probably get the local PD involved too."

"Yep, go ahead and have a couple units come to our location." Renz ended the call and dialed Taft, who said she'd send the PD and our agents to the mayor's mansion immediately.

Chapter 51

We backed out of the bedroom to avoid contaminating the scene. I offered to stay behind while Renz and Tommy canvassed the neighborhood to ask if anyone had seen suspicious characters or heard unusual noises last night or early that morning. I watched out the window for the police to show up. Our forensic team and either Dave Mann or a tech from the medical examiner's office would take longer to arrive.

I paced back and forth in the living room. It was obvious that the killers of now fourteen people were all one and the same. It had to be a fairly large group in order to have someone available anytime day or night to commit the violent murders that had taken place over the last five days. That number stuck in my mind.

Why is five a common denominator in those murders? Five homeless people killed, five loved ones of people connected to the mayor killed, today is the fifth day from the initial murders, and the fifth of May was when something happened that started this shitshow in motion.

My mind flashed back to the newspaper article I saw

yesterday when we were searching the archives. I hadn't read beyond the headlines, but I remembered the article was written several days after May fifth. "Damn!"

Maybe the seventh or eighth?

It was about five siblings who'd drowned in a lake, but I hadn't read where the drownings took place or what the victims' names were. I needed to find that article and read it.

Dave would know. He's the medical examiner.

I called his cell phone even though I knew he was probably driving to our location or to the attorney's house. Thankfully, he answered right away.

"Dave Mann here."

"Dave, it's Jade. I have a super important question to ask you, and you're going to have to remember back to May."

"Okay, I'll do my best, but can't it wait? I'll be at your location in ten minutes."

"You're coming here?"

"Yes, I thought there was a dead body there."

"I'm sorry. Yes, there is. I didn't know if you were coming to our location or the other one."

"Oh, well, what do you need to know that can't wait for, now, eight minutes?"

"Only one thing until you get here."

"Shoot."

"Do you remember the drowning incident of those five siblings in May, and were the bodies brought to your office?"

"Yes and yes. It was a tragic accident. They were trapped

in the family vehicle, and none of them were able to escape."

"Are you able to access those reports on the computer in your van?"

"Yes, I am."

"Okay, that's all I need to know until you get here. Thanks."

That had to be it. The death of those five brothers and sisters had to be the reason for all the murders—it was revenge, retaliation, whatever one wanted to call it. The mayor must have caused the accident but only if it actually happened on the night of May fifth in that short two-mile distance between Silver Shores Resort and the mayor's estate. I pulled up the map of the city on my phone, looked for a lake in that area, and found one. It wasn't a large lake, but all that was necessary was for it to be deep enough to submerge a vehicle and drown everyone inside. I was about to look for the article online when two squad cars screeched to a stop in front of the house. I had to pocket my phone and address the situation at hand.

The officers banged on the front door, and I turned the knob with my sleeve and allowed them in. Gloves were plentiful in the cruiser, but I needed to remain inside until Renz and Tommy were back. I showed the officers my ID and led them to the master suite, where Julie's body lay.

"The medical examiner and forensic team are en route. Go ahead and give the perimeter a thorough look, scour the street, and wrap the yard in tape."

"Yes, ma'am."

I nodded a thanks, and as I watched out the window for

Dave, I saw Renz and Tommy on the opposite side of the street, knocking on doors.

Minutes later, the medical examiner's van pulled up to the curb. All I needed Dave to do was show me how to access the family's records if he was even permitted to do that. If not, he might remember or could personally look up the date he'd written down as his best guess for a time of death.

I stood at the front door and waited while he got his supplies from the back of the van. Dave approached me with a head tip.

"She's right this way," I said. "Any idea when Forensics will show up?"

"They're about ten minutes behind me."

"Then we have a little time, right? They have to take pictures before you move the body."

He scratched his head. "What do you need to know about those drownings, Jade?"

"Where that lake was and when you called the time of death. Also, the family's last name."

He sighed. "Okay, let's go back to the van so I can look it up. I can't let you access the records yourself, but I can email you the autopsy reports."

"That's all I need, and I sure appreciate it."

I stood at the curb and kept silent while Dave logged on to his records database and looked up the information.

"Okay, here we go. It's harder to determine TOD in drowning cases, but you know that."

I nodded.

"I went by what the parents told me as in when the kids were expected back from church camp. They were supposed to be home on the night of May fifth, but they didn't show. My autopsy report reflects that the TOD for the kids could fit in that two-day time frame. They were discovered on the afternoon of May seventh."

My heart pounded harder. "And where were they discovered?"

"South of Atwater Park. There's a large pond on the west side of the road, but it's deep enough to completely submerge a vehicle."

"Is there any notation of what happened to that van?"

"Those kind of records would be archived at the police department."

I knew that to be true but wondered why I'd never heard that tragic story. I assumed I was on an out-of-state case at the time. "And the family name?"

"The parents are Jacob and Evelyn Ashton, and they live on the east side."

"Okay, thanks, Dave."

"Yep, and I've sent the reports to your email address."

I glanced up when I heard a vehicle slow to a stop. Our forensic team had just arrived. I shielded my eyes and looked up and down the street for Renz and Tommy. I didn't see either of them, so I called Renz's cell phone.

"Hey, partner, why don't you guys come back to Julie's house? I think I've figured out the case."

"You did what? Okay, we're on our way."

Chapter 52

While Dave addressed Julie's body and the forensic team processed the house, I sat on the stoop with Tommy and Renz and explained my theory. Dave had already sent the autopsy reports to my email, and everything began to make sense, except now we didn't have Julie or Doug to pit against each other about the events from the night of May fifth.

Renz rubbed his forehead. "So you think the mayor somehow caused that van to go off the road into the lake, and now the parents are on a killing rampage? It seems like a lot for people pushing fifty to accomplish."

"They obviously had young people working with them. There was Brandon and Erik as well as Cole and Lucas."

"Why wouldn't they just go public with it, and how would they have known the mayor was involved to begin with?" Tommy asked.

"That's where I'm stuck. Dave said the bodies weren't discovered until May seventh, but don't forget, the mayor's car was repaired on May sixth. The parents must have reported the kids missing, yet that still doesn't implicate the mayor. Without proof of wrongdoing, it's just coincidental timing. We need to talk to Michael Kent directly, and I'd say we ought to do that immediately. If he was involved in a cover-up and now he's in danger, we need to know that. Somebody, and most likely the parents of those five dead kids, are probably going after him next. Julie and Doug, his possible co-conspirators, are dead, and now he's the final person to eliminate—the coup de grâce."

Renz fished his phone from his pocket. "I need to call Taft right away. Carl and Mike can question the mayor if they're at the mansion and he's coherent, or they can bring him to the police station for safekeeping, sober him up, and question him there while we pay Mr. and Mrs. Ashton a visit."

Renz made the call to Taft while we waited. I saw from the expression on his face and the fact that he instantly went white that something was terribly wrong. My eyes were locked with his, then he passed his phone to me. "Taft needs to speak with you."

"What? Why?"

"Just take the phone, Jade."

I put the phone up to my ear and said hello. What Taft told me nearly caused me to faint. I couldn't think, I couldn't speak, and I didn't know what to do.

I remembered Renz taking me by the arm and running with me to the cruiser.

"Come on, Jade! Snap out of it. You're an FBI agent, so get your head in the game. We've got to go! Tommy, you're driving. Head to the mayor's mansion as fast as you can."

Renz sat in the back seat with me and tried to calm me down. I was nearing hysteria, and my thoughts were scattered in a million directions.

"Why, Renz? Why do they have Amber? What on earth would they want her for? I can't lose another family member to violence. She doesn't know them—I don't even know them! What do they want with us?"

"I don't know, Jade, but they said they want you and only you, or they'll kill her. SWAT is on the way. You were right, it's Jacob and Evelyn Ashton. They've got the mayor, his wife, and Amber held hostage. Taft said they're blaming the FBI for interfering in their mission, and they mentioned you specifically."

"Because I was doing my job?"

"I don't know, but I can't let you go in alone. Right now, everyone is being held at the gate. They were told that Jacob and Evelyn will kill Amber, Michael, and Marie if anyone other than you comes in."

"I was reckless. It's my fault they have Amber. I taunted them with that jacket and had you take a picture of me and Cole with it. I followed the bus to Barclay Street and ended up getting punched in the face that night. They obviously knew everything about me and followed me home."

"Shh. We need to focus on right now, on this moment. Amber is counting on you."

The SWAT team arrived within minutes and tried to take over the situation.

"There's no way I'm going to let you jeopardize my sister's life. They want to talk to me, they're watching us from the house, and I'm going to comply. I need to know what really happened, so don't try to stop me. If you can think of a back way to get in, then go ahead, but don't you dare do anything that's going to risk my sister's life!"

I walked to the gate's call box, pressed the button, and waited. Seconds later, a woman's voice answered.

"Who's there?"

"This is Agent Jade Monroe. Who am I speaking to? I know Marie's voice, and you aren't her."

"Hold your ID badge toward the camera so I can see it."

I did as ordered and was pretty certain I was speaking with Evelyn Ashton. "Is this Evelyn?"

Renz gave me a thumbs-up. He knew I had regained my composure, and I needed to do what an FBI agent would logically do to save my sister. I also knew that SWAT's agenda was to save the mayor, but if I was lucky, I could talk the couple down and save all three of them.

"This is Evelyn. Sounds like you've done your homework, Jade Monroe. Too bad you weren't smart enough to know we'd go after one of your loved ones too. We have to make the guilty parties feel the pain we felt when the mayor killed our children."

"Mrs. Ashton, how do you know the mayor caused their deaths?" That was the burning question we needed answers to, and I hoped she would give me a reason while the police and my teammates were there to hear her.

"I confronted him myself. I'm the one who came upon the accident on my way home from work that night. He was as drunk as a skunk and barely conscious while he sat there in his damaged BMW. I asked if he was okay, and he said he had people coming to help him. I thought I recognized the man and took a picture of his license plate before I left." I heard Evelyn's sobs through the intercom. "I couldn't wait to get home to my kids, who had been at church camp for two weeks. I pass that spot every day on my way to and from work, but after I realized our children were missing, I didn't give that man another thought. It wasn't until two days later that I stopped at that very place where he sat drunk in his car on the night of May fifth. That's when I saw it."

I looked at my teammates, and they shook their heads. All I wanted to do was get to Amber, but the SWAT team insisted I keep Evelyn talking so they could find another way in.

"What did you see, Evelyn?"

"I saw the ruts in the ground from the tires. I walked to the water's edge, and three feet beneath the surface was the van's roof."

She suddenly stopped talking, and a man's voice came over the speaker. "Come inside now or your sister dies. You're stalling, and we know it. I'm opening the gate, but if anyone else enters, all three of them will die, and their blood will be on your hands. Leave your weapon outside the gate and no funny stuff. You know what we're capable of."

The iron gates creaked ominously as they opened. I needed to suck up my fears and anxiety and get Amber out safely. I would do what I could for the mayor and his wife, but I was only one person, and Amber was my main concern. My sister's life depended on me having a clear head and my wits about me. If SWAT could rescue the mayor, then they should but not by risking Amber's life. I walked through the open gate and looked back at Renz. "I won't let them kill Amber, no matter what it takes."

"Jade, I'm going with SWAT. If I can find a way in, I'll come to you. I'm not leaving you in there alone."

I placed my gun on the ground, pulled in a deep breath, and continued toward the mansion.

Chapter 53

When I finally reached the massive front door, I pressed the brass lever and pushed the door inward. Since I had been there before, I knew where several of the first-floor rooms were located. I crossed the tiled foyer, looked left and right, and saw them in the library. My heart was in my throat, but I needed to remain calm. I finally put eyes on the people responsible for nearly fifteen murders.

The number five filled my mind again. It all stemmed from having five children who'd died on May fifth, and although my heart broke for them, nobody was above the law. They'd crossed into a place even more dangerous—they had hostages—and that told me their lives didn't mean much to them anymore.

"Come toward us with your fingers locked above your head, Agent Monroe."

I was looking into the eyes of a broken and desperate man who had nothing to lose, and there was no telling what he or Evelyn might do.

I jerked my chin toward another man who I wasn't expecting to see. "Who's he?"

"He's our helper for the day, Micah."

Amber squirmed in the chair she was bound to. I shook my head. "Stay calm, Sis. Please, stay calm."

"Good advice, Jade. You do know why we have your sister, don't you?" Evelyn asked.

"Yes. You needed to right the wrongs, and I disrupted your plans. Why didn't you go to the authorities and tell them what you saw?"

Evelyn spewed her contempt for the law at me. "I looked up the license plate I took a picture of and saw who it belonged to. I called the mayor's office and confronted him on the phone. That was the only time he spoke to me. His 'people' handled us, denied everything, and said the mayor was never there, I was mistaken, and that the mayor's car was in perfect condition. I had the wrong man. They also said if I tried to blame him publicly for anything, they'd ruin our lives, sue us for slandering the mayor, and destroy our credibility. They broke into our home, stole my phone with the picture of his license plate on it, and took our computer. My husband is an online minister to people who are shut-ins. They threatened to make up lies about him and ruin his reputation." Evelyn jabbed the bound mayor with her finger. "He murdered my family because he's nothing but a rich drunken son of a bitch. He needs to pay with his life. An eye for an eye!"

"Let my sister go. She has nothing to do with the pain you're feeling," I said. "I'll stay. I'll do whatever I can to help you. If the mayor is responsible for your family's tragic death, I'll make sure a full investigation begins immediately.

We have records of his comings and goings that night. We know where he was, and witnesses have said he was drunk when he left the event he was at. It doesn't matter that he's the mayor—he isn't above the law either."

"We're nobody, and we won't be believed. People will think we made up everything and want an enormous settlement because the Kent's are wealthy." Jacob nodded to Micah, who slammed his fist into the mayor's face.

"No, stop!" I pleaded with them. "We can work this out. I promise you I'll do everything I can to help."

"It's too late. We'll never get a fair trial in this city. I want to be with my children." Evelyn lifted the gun that sat next to her on Michael Kent's desk. It took but a split second for her to raise it to her head and pull the trigger.

I screamed when Jacob shot the mayor with his own gun and pulled back Amber's head. Everything was spiraling out of control.

"You've interfered in our lives, Agent Monroe. We could have completed our mission and moved on, but now, not only are my children dead, but my wife is dead too!"

He exposed a large knife and brought it to Amber's throat just as an explosion of gunfire erupted with echoes bouncing off the coffered ceiling. Jacob fell to the floor, blood streaming from his head wounds.

Renz rushed into the room with his gun pointed at Micah. He ordered him to the ground as the SWAT team entered and took him into custody. I ran to Amber's side, and as I untied her, Renz reached us. "Are you okay?"

Amber nodded as I pulled the tape from her mouth, and

then I hugged her with everything I had. Renz pulled the bindings off Marie and helped her to her feet.

"How did you get in, Renz? You saved Amber's life."

"We'll talk later. Let's get them outside."

Chapter 54

A week had passed since that horrific day, and I counted every blessing I had. Amber was safe, I was safe, and so were my teammates. I'd thanked Renz dozens of times until he finally told me to knock it off—in his words, he was only doing his job. I knew better.

We'd made a deal with Marie—Michael would be buried with dignity and the attention any city official deserved, and the story would be that burglars had broken into their mansion and shot him. At a later date and under the guise of spending time in Europe, Marie would serve time in a woman's prison for covering up five deaths caused by her husband. How much time she would serve, I didn't know, and I had no say in that. Nobody was a winner in that case, and as much as it bothered me that the mayor was buried with pomp and circumstance as an upstanding city official, I wasn't the one making the deals. Life would go on, we'd continue to do our job to the best of our ability, and I could only hope that honest, hard-working people got a fair shake during their years on earth. It was the best I or anybody else in my profession could do.

I'd warned Renz that if he thought I was bad about thanking him, Amber was far worse. She wouldn't leave him alone until she gave him a proper thank-you for saving her life. He was responsible for her now, according to the ancient proverb, whether he liked it or not. I teased him about that.

The day after the shooting at the mayor's mansion, Renz explained to me how he'd ended up being the one who got to us first. It was only because he had been in the home before and knew how the rooms were laid out on the first floor. He and the SWAT team had gotten in through the cellar window after scaling the side wall with the team's climbing equipment. Renz cut away from the group and found his way up the stairs through the wine cellar. He knew the library was straight ahead, and when he heard my voice, he followed it—and with the grace of God, got to us just in time.

"So what will make Amber happy?" he asked after watching part of the mayor's funeral on TV during our lunch hour. I had no desire to attend the service.

I smiled. "Well, since you don't really know much about Amber's cooking skills other than the doughnuts she made to rival the delicious ones at Gold Nugget Café in Central City, she wants you over for dinner."

"That's it? That's an easy task."

"Not really since there will be plenty of them you'll have to attend. For the first one, you have to create the menu yourself, a four-course meal, and it has to be whatever your heart desires."

Renz frowned. "But I'm a simple guy and don't even know what's included in a four-course meal."

"An hors d'oeuvre, appetizer, the main course, and dessert. Easy peasy, but it has to be your favorite food."

"I'm Spanish. I like burritos and tamales."

"Okay, no problem. Amber can make any kind of food on earth, and I promise it'll be delicious. Grab that napkin, and I'll help you with the rest." I squeezed Renz's arm with forever gratitude. "Oh, and just so you know, for dessert, I'm a big fan of sweet cream-cheese-filled sopaipilla bars."

He smiled. "Duly noted."

THE END

Thank you!

Thanks for reading *Blood Reckoning*, the third book in the FBI Agent Jade Monroe Live or Die Series. I hope you enjoyed it!

Find all my books leading up to this series at http://cmsutter.com

Stay abreast of my new releases by signing up for my VIP email list at: http://cmsutter.com/newsletter/

You'll be one of the first to get a glimpse of the cover reveals and release dates, and you'll have a chance at exciting raffles offered with each new release.

Posting a review will help other readers find my books. I appreciate every review, whether positive or negative, and if you have a second to spare, a review is truly appreciated.

Find me on Facebook at https://www.facebook.com/cmsutterauthor/

Made in the USA
Las Vegas, NV
01 May 2023

71400020R00166